THE ORWELL BRIGADE

THE ORWELL BRIGADE

John Burdett
John Lantigua
Ernesto Mallo
Matt Rees
Colin Cotterill
Quentin Bates

Mike Lawson
Gary Phillips
Ruth Dudley Edwards
Christopher G. Moore
Barbara Nadel
George Fetherling

Edited by Christopher G. Moore

Heaven Lake Press

Distributed in Thailand by:
Asia Document Bureau Ltd.
P.O. Box 1029
Nana Post Office
Bangkok 10112 Thailand
Fax: (662) 260-4578
www.heavenlakepress.com
email: editorial@heavenlakepress.com

Book copyright © 2012 Asia Document Bureau Ltd.
Individual story copyright © 2012 the authors: *Orwell, the Man Who Said No in Thunder* by John Burdett, *JOE—2012* by Mike Lawson, *The Boulevard of Dreams and Nightmares: When Rich and Poor Live on the Same Street* by John Lantigua, *Wading While Black, Suspects in Fact and Crime Fiction* by Gary Phillips, *One in Any Given Night* by Ernesto Mallo, *Orwell and the IRA* by Ruth Dudley Edwards, *Doublethink for the Arab Spring* by Matt Rees, *Killing Fields Justice: A Witness to History* by Christopher G. Moore, *Jai Yen* by Colin Cotterill, *Transformation* by Barbara Nadel, *Emerging from the Crash* by Quentin Bates, *Shaking the Hand that Shook the Hand: A Footnote to Orwell* by George Fetherling

First published in Thailand in 2012
by Heaven Lake Press

Jacket design: Colin Cotterill

ISBN 978-616-7503-16-5

Contents

Introduction	ix
Orwell, the Man Who Said No in Thunder by John Burdett	1
JOE—2012 by Mike Lawson	9
The Boulevard of Dreams and Nightmares: When Rich and Poor Live on the Same Street by John Lantigua	21
Wading While Black, Suspects in Fact and Crime Fiction by Gary Phillips	29
One in Any Given Night by Ernesto Mallo	49
Orwell and the IRA by Ruth Dudley Edwards	57
Doublethink for the Arab Spring by Matt Rees	71
Killing Fields Justice: A Witness to History by Christopher G. Moore	85
Jai Yen by Colin Cotterill	103
Transformation by Barbara Nadel	119
Emerging from the Crash by Quentin Bates	139
Shaking the Hand that Shook the Hand: A Footnote to Orwell by George Fetherling	155

"Journalism is printing what someone else does not want printed; everything else is public relations."
—George Orwell

Introduction
Authenticity, Politics and Writing

What is Orwell's legacy? And why should we care, more than sixty years after his death?

The simple answer is Orwell's worldview transcended his time. He warned in his novels and essays how the surveillance state was fundamentally incompatible with democracy. What he had to say about the abuse of official power in his essays remains relevant for us and for those around us. This is not the ephemeral content of a daily news cycle. An essay that stands the test of time reminds us that the best qualities of writing are universal, truthful—a workbench with tools of perception that we can use to judge our own lives, issues of war and peace, the role of government and political decisions that set perimeters around our range of options.

Reviving the tradition of the novelist/essayist in the Orwell tradition could be one way of keeping those in power honest, accountable and actionable. Lying is a not just a way of political life; it is a way to control people's interests, desires, motives, and memories. Fear is something Orwell faced. He didn't run away. Neither should we.

Orwell's *A Hanging* and *Shooting an Elephant*, personal accounts of his time as a low-ranking colonial official during the British administration of Burma, are remarkable and memorable firsthand essays. Here was a

Introduction

writer who, by writing about what he had experienced, managed to shape, hone and refine the heated emotions of his day. The essays remind us that often matters come down to the basics of a hanging and shooting. The condemned man being marched to the gallows is suddenly, unexpectedly mindful of a puddle in his path and does the most human of things: he steps around it so as not to spoil his shoes.

In *Homage to Catalonia*, in which he drew upon his six months of fighting during the Spanish Civil War, Orwell wrote:

> It was the first time that I had seen a person whose profession was telling lies—unless one counts journalists.

What troubled Orwell the most, having been at the front line in Barcelona, was how the British press used falsehood, rumors and distortions to describe the events. War coverage in Barcelona was written to pander to the left wing in England. Anyone who has witnessed violence near a front line will understand the fluid nature of perception when it comes to such an experience, the choice of one detail over another in accounting for it afterward and the careless disconnect between events, their retelling and their meaning. But those far removed from the front could smile in disdain at Orwell's anger.

The war reporting we see today follows a similar script to what Orwell found in Spain. The media and the press are little different, little improved since Orwell's time. However, we live in a more wired, interconnected and cynical world than Orwell's. It has made many of us numb to a steady stream of images showing murder, brutality and destruction, accompanied by endless lies and duplicity. What shocked and outraged Orwell has become a normal part of our daily lives.

In these essays questions of sensitivity, flawed moral compasses, disparities of power, and the roles of unrestrained wealth and brutality suggest the intractability of issues that are little changed from Orwell's time. We still haven't discovered a method to solve these issues. For many, the road ahead appears narrower. The feeling of helplessness leads people to settle for reduced liberties and freedom, drawing the curtain on hope for meaningful change. Orwell thought the benefits of such a trade-off were an illusion; he believed one couldn't live free inside a totalitarian system.

We are entering an age where this disagreement about the nature of freedom inside a rigged political space is being put to the test. Today there is less consensus than there was in Orwell's time about which regimes are totalitarian and which are free, just as we disagree more than ever about the meaning and scope of freedom. And in Orwell's day the globalized corporate world and big international media had yet to come into the picture.

Scandals like the phone hacking by reporters at the *News of the World* have caused us to question "facts," "reality" and "truth telling." While corporate espionage—including data mining—is a worry, this threat pales against that of large corporate and government efforts to shape facts and reality.

We have become less innocent about the way the corporate media use images and words to "sell" a commercial or political position. At the same time, from Africa to Asia, Europe to the Americas, examples are multiplying where regimes employ totalitarian tools, justifications and attitudes while at the same time claiming "freedom" prevails. In the United States the Espionage

Introduction

Act has been used against whistle-blowers who shine a light on government wrongdoing and cover-ups, along with the vast unregulated expansion of covert surveillance on phone calls, emails and social networks. Such activities make a mockery of the constitutional limits on search and seizure, as do executive orders authorizing the assassination of citizens. An undeclared war on dissent has become an endless battle on many fronts waged in cyberspace. Today, most countries deploy their cyber-troops to locate, identify, block, threaten, harass, and close down the new enemies whose opinions contradict the official position or version.

This digital battleground isn't one that Orwell faced. You can't read the news without finding a casualty report dispatched from somewhere along the front lines of this battle. Most often such articles—in state controlled media—are lopsided accounts to show how the government's policies have been created for the public good. Such propaganda depends on the effectiveness of government officials who patrol cyberspace, monitor and neutralize leaks, dissent or challenges that might establish the direct and indirect connections that exist between the economic elites and the elite political class.

As we retreat into our computer screens, we discover that our freedom of expression and our security in the world have been downgraded to below junk bond quality. This desperate state of affairs is dictating our collective new assignment in the surveillance state. Every generation has to claim the world back for truth telling. It doesn't happen on autopilot. And Orwell was a very experienced "pilot" who worked in coal mines, lived rough in Paris, and fought in a civil war. We haven't yet come to terms with the fact that, although we know we live in a surveillance state, this is only the beginning of a more pervasive and effective ecology that herds us into a fictive monoculture where no one can escape the watching, assembling, analyzing, storing, distributing, and modeling of their personal information.

Technology will have many more tools waiting to ambush our freedoms in the future. What Orwell feared has, in many respects, come to pass. The role of contemporary authors will be to carry forward Orwell's fight for freedom to speak out against the doublespeak and newspeak.

In *Nineteen Eighty-Four*, Orwell described a country he called Oceania, a regime founded on rewriting history. By controlling the past, Oceania's truth keepers and timeline owners control the present and guide it into a future of their own devising. This power to upload a new reality was the nightmare, the horror of *Nineteen Eighty-Four*.

Finding a voice that allowed him a way to turn politics into literature, Orwell handed down a warning for our time, perhaps all times:

> Looking at the world as a whole, the drift for many decades has been not towards anarchy but towards the reimposition of slavery. We may be heading not for general breakdown but for an epoch as horribly stable as the slave empires of antiquity.

The engine of the new slavery is capitalism, which is not evolving into a new and different system but stays eternally the same. Greed-driven, capitalism is an acquiring, extractive and exploitative system that finds, takes, alters, and distributes resources to maximize gain and then allocate wealth to a tiny few. Unless restrained, it becomes a doomsday machine, devouring

Introduction

and unstoppable. There are no saints of denial fighting in the capitalist trenches. There are only slaves seeking to escape, and that is difficult if not impossible in a surveillance state.

Our innate greed has found the perfect vehicle in which to race ahead, as if a breakneck rate of change will inevitably deliver us to a better future. Capitalism at this late stage comes down to a coin flip: heads, technology will rescue us from a system hell-bent on assisting us in our own destruction, or tails, technology will accelerate our demise. And we won't really know the winner of the toss until it's too late to ask for the best of two out of three.

While that coin is still in the air, you have time to read the essays in *The Orwell Brigade* and spend a few hours among a group of truth tellers who seek to preserve the spirit of George Orwell. We are novelists, but we also share a vision that writers should use their passion, talents and experience to address political issues—issues that, it turns out, differ little from those of Orwell's day. In plain words we draw on some of the great Orwellian themes of our times: the economic collapse in America and Europe, a trend for capitalism and totalitarian elites to find common ground, anti-rational/anti-science populists who use religion to push back the Enlightenment, the growing inequality among citizens of all countries and the rise of new technological means of control, surveillance and destruction as Ministries of Truth roam the Internet on behalf of many governments in a way that Orwell could never have foreseen.

In *Nineteen Eighty-Four* Winston Smith, taken to the dreaded Room 101 for memory replacement, learns that two plus two can equal five. Room 101 is a metaphor for the final destination of all of us who fail to speak plainly about the distortions in the relationship between those who cling to power and those who hunger to replace them, while the rest of us are wedged in the war zone in between.

It would be a mistake to believe that today's intellectuals are any less committed than those in the past. But one problem today is the amount of noise rattling around silos of big data. Informational noise muffles the modern-day Orwellian voice. People like the feel-good buzz of connectedness, logging into the very technology governments and large corporation use to control and shape their thoughts. We have never had better access to the means of communication. We have never had institutions with better tools to monitor and censor what we can watch and what we can say, and better means to flood the communication channels with their own "truth" about the meaning of events.

In *The Orwell Brigade* a dozen novelists from various corners of the world—Quentin Bates, John Burdett, Colin Cotterill, Ruth Dudley Edwards, George Fetherling, John Lantigua, Mike Lawson, Ernesto Mallo, Barbara Nadel, Gary Phillips, Matt Rees and I—have set aside the task of writing fiction to produce an essay. Most of our essays are firsthand accounts of the Orwellian world of our age, focusing on contemporary social justice issues ranging from social inequality increasingly widened as political institutions become dysfunctional, to persistent racism and discrimination against minorities, to memories of state tyranny and war crimes and political thugs at their games of corruption, to intimidation and killings in sectarian strife.

In this volume you will find political essays that dissect the posturing, cant and hypocrisy that survives, mutates

Introduction

and is passed along as part of each generational change. Our essays are a tribute to the legacy of George Orwell, who never gave up the writer's obligation of telling truth to power.

John Burdett's *Orwell, the Man Who Said No in Thunder* explores how Orwell refused to play the game of colonial empire and how since his death the totalitarianism of money has seeded a new global empire.

Mike Lawson's *JOE—2012* imagines J. Edgar Hoover in 2012, running the new surveillance society of America by plugging into the latest high technology to watch citizens and keep records on everyone in the grand tradition of Big Brother.

John Lantigua's *The Boulevard of Dreams and Nightmares: When Rich and Poor Live on the Same Street* examines the growing poverty in places like Florida and how inequality has divided a nation by class, race and education, leaving vast areas of unemployed and hopeless people.

Gary Phillips's *Wading While Black, Suspects in Fact and Crime Fiction* transports us to the world of racism in the media, the police, the courts, and political institutions in America and relates how black crime authors have battled to escape the ghetto of racism and prejudice.

Ernesto Mallo's *One in Any Given Night* explores the methods the torturers and dictators used during the years of totalitarianism in Argentina—more than a decade of mass imprisonment, disappearance, terror, and death—and how they justified and enriched themselves.

Ruth Dudley Edwards's *Orwell and the IRA* takes on the long, troubled history of Ireland and Northern Ireland and of the IRA as it took on the role of Big Brother.

Matt Rees's *Doublethink for the Arab Spring* is a disturbing look inside Gaza, where local gangsters who co-opt the political process carry out ruthless assassinations as they adopt Orwellian excuses for their cold-blooded murder.

My essay, titled *Killing Fields Justice: A Witness to History*, chronicles the context of opening day at the Khmer Rouge Tribunal as the leaders of what was a prime example of an Orwellian regime went on trial for the genocide they organized and carried out in Cambodia in the 1970s.

Colin Cotterill's *Jai Yen* tackles the Orwellian world of Burmese migrants living in Thailand. The politics of schooling at the local level reveals how a practical solution can find a way around the prejudice and official barriers that would deny children an education.

Barbara Nadel's *Transformation* transports us to Turkey and inside the Orwellian world of nationalistic militarism and the long history of discrimination against homosexual, bisexual and, in particular, transgendered people.

Quentin Bates's *Emerging from the Crash* looks at the combination of power, corruption and propaganda inside the political and economic establishment of Iceland.

George Fetherling's *Shaking the Hand that Shook the Hand: A Footnote to Orwell* examines how the legacy of Orwell has been passed down from one generation to the next by looking at the friendship of George Orwell and George Woodcock.

George Orwell's legacy consists of more than his razor sharp perceptions about the tools and techniques governments use to oppress their citizens. His essays are testimonials to an author's courage to speak out during a time when many of the outspoken lapsed into silence, fearing the powerful would be displeased. During Orwell's time totalitarian regimes were largely based on communist

Introduction

ideology. In modern times totalitarian regimes are more likely based on a cult of personality or a religious ideology. The defeat of communism as an alternative ideology has not delivered freedom but only new ways for totalitarian institutions to remain in positions of power. One purpose of this volume of essays is to bring readers up to date with the techniques, methods and technology of the modern Orwellian world—the one in which repressive regimes are discovering that new technology offers new opportunities to use secrecy, surveillance, disinformation, and intimidation to retain power and suppress dissent.

Fiction usually arrives with an author's disclaimer that none of what happens in the book really happened, and that none of the characters are based on actual people. The events in these essays happened, and the people whose lives were affected are real. The essays expose and reveal the full weight of government and corporate power, the structure and administration of that authority, and the consequences to freedom and liberties. The corners of the world described are only parts of the bigger story that lies behind the public relations machine piloted by governments, media and large corporations. We are all passengers taking a ride, or being taken for a ride. And as you fasten your seatbelts and look around at the others on this long flight, have a think about where, in the end, we will land, and when we disembark, what we will find. It may be waiting for us not only in the shadows, but in broad daylight.

Christopher G. Moore
Bangkok, Thailand
October 30, 2012

Orwell, the Man Who Said No in Thunder

John Burdett

As a colonial policeman in Burma, George Orwell found himself in the awkward position of having to kill an elephant. The awkwardness came not from any lack of courage—you will be hard put to find a braver man in the annals of English literature—but from the fact that the poor elephant was not threatening anyone. It was not a rampaging tusker in masth but simply another creature, like man, who preferred freedom to chains. When Orwell found it, the elephant was calmly throwing leaves and dust over itself with its trunk. The reason for shooting it was what, all over Asia, is known as "face." As the white man on the scene, he had to—well, play the white man. Which he did, and was duly applauded by the "natives." In the midst of his self-loathing, he knew the murder of the elephant was a minor enactment of a drama that had been playing all over the Earth for three hundred years: to keep their face, the British had to demonstrate that, having colonised half the world with all the brutality that an industrialised economy can muster against the non-industrialised, they would now use that brutality to protect their victims, even to the extreme of snuffing a harmless elephant. It was the kind of protection racket any mafia don would recognise.

There is a "frisson" at the centre of every great writer, a clash of tectonic plates in the inner world of the personality, which produces the energy—and the absolute necessity—to write. Here, in the story of the elephant, Orwell reveals with clinical self-awareness the nature of his internal torment: he was killing one of nature's wonders for the sake of a hypocritical piece of showmanship, but he didn't *want* to be a hypocrite. He didn't want to *play up and play the game*, as they were still telling us it was our British duty to do when I was a schoolboy. He was by no means alone in this. Many, if not most, of the finest minds in England had grave doubts about the empire on which the sun refused to set, doubts not only on behalf of its foreign subjects, but concerning the effect unlimited power has on those who wield it. If it is true that absolute power corrupts absolutely, then the corruption of the British mind by Orwell's day was pretty much absolute. We no longer walked; as an entire nation we strutted—not a few still do. Orwell preferred a more honourable destiny.

As all modern economists agree, the empire was fuelled by slavery and opium sales (true, slavery was banned in the early nineteenth century in the UK, but that did not stop us buying cotton from Virginia at slave-cheap prices). Orwell's father was himself a certified trafficker in opium on behalf of Her Majesty Queen Victoria, so Orwell experienced the nausea close up and personal. Almost any other man would have compromised with his conscience and told himself it wasn't his fault he was born white, British and middle-class, and why not accept the benefits—which, in terms of the opportunities available to most of the rest of the world, were considerable? Not Eric Blair, for that was his real name. On the contrary, the six-foot-two Englishman with the floppy hair went out of his way to turn himself into one of life's victims, for his demon would not have it any other way. Although he was never seriously poor, he dragged himself around the odious doss-houses of Paris and London at a time when such places were fetid, disease-ridden (he caught his tuberculosis in one of them) and hardly an inch above prisons in social status. As a socialist he was not content with the comfortable life of a left-wing London intellectual. He went down the mines at Wigan and told it like it really was—quite a revelation for Marxist Bloomsbury, which rarely rubbed shoulders with the proletariat they championed. And he went to Spain and joined the International Brigade to fight against Franco. It was an irony typical of his life that his experience as a colonial policeman qualified him to train and lead a ragged band of revolutionaries in the freezing hills of Catalonia, where he barely survived a bullet in the neck. And it was typical of his ruthless honesty that he quickly became disillusioned with communism and said so loud and clear. *Animal Farm* was the product of his loathing for all forms of totalitarianism, especially of the Stalinist kind. Then, at the end of his short life, when he was dying of tuberculosis, came the absolute disillusionment that alone can produce the absolute masterpiece: his *King Lear* is called *Nineteen Eighty-Four*. He wrote it in an isolated, freezing cottage on the wild coast of Jura Island in the Hebrides, where the post arrived twice a week, weather permitting.

I suppose today there are untold numbers of Englishmen and women whose souls are so hollowed out by gadgets, alcohol, football and *EastEnders* that George Orwell, if they have heard of him at all, appears to them as a clown figure, someone who burned while Rome fiddled. After all, we defeated totalitarianism worldwide, didn't we?

Personally, I don't think so. What I see is a new form of totalitarianism which needs no particular identity or charter, which needs no propaganda and which is everywhere, like a mutation of Big Brother. Call it the Totalitarianism of Money (TOM). I am not a religious person, but it seems to me the world's religions can take credit for one thing. Throughout recorded history, up until recently, religions provided both a physical and an all-important psychic space where anyone—anyone at all—could find some relief from the overwhelming burden of materialism. The divine dictum that "Man shall not live by bread alone" is only a partial answer to the devil's question "How do you turn stones into bread?" but it does give partial relief. Now that sacred space is being eroded all over the world. Sure, you may still enter a church and pray for inner peace, but your creditors, the taxman, the mortgage company, the costs of education, peer pressure, and unpleasant messages on your smart phone will enter with you in your head. Priests, monks and shamans have no power that can stand up to TOM. And don't even think about psychiatrists, antidepressants or trained counsellors—that stuff costs money. Do the noble thing and raise your moral profile by dedicating yourself to the next generation? Forget it; TOM is there already in the price of all the must-haves, which include electronic toys for five-year-olds and up. One hundred thousand years of empirical evidence proves that children do not need electronic toys, but try telling that to your peer-pressured seven-year-old who demands an iPad to compete. TOM has stolen the most important half of parenthood, for we are allowing him to mould our children's minds and brains. Clean air and water, too, are only to be had at a price—in the case of air, quite a high one since you'll need to live in the Alps or the Himalayas. And if you and your family are sensitive to noise and street crime and require a quiet life? Well, you'd better have enough dough to buy a home in a gated community with strict rules.

How did this happen? I was educated up to degree level and beyond without my parents having to pay a penny ("education" in those days meant a study in the apprehension of reality, rather than how to become one of TOM's better-paid apostles). I drank water straight from the tap, got free shots for all the usual diseases. Everywhere was quiet after about eight p.m., and people judged one another for character rather than bank balance. There was virtually no street crime except in small pockets in the city's badlands, and even that was rarely violent.

So why don't we do something about it at the next election? Are you kidding? Elections are bought and sold through Wall Street and the City. Is TOM going to allow his high priests to fund a campaign against him? No way, José. And José might just be the name of TOM's favourite fixer, for they say about a third of the world's money is laundered. TOM is having a great time in Mexico sending his foot soldiers to their hideous deaths while the overlords, who are intimately connected with, if not senior members of, government and law enforcement, are loyally bringing in the pesos. Legalise it? Curious that TOM-funded politicians worldwide have come out against that genuine silver bullet that would stop the violence—and the flow of dough—in an instant, as it did in the days of Prohibition and Al Capone. And did you hear what Jamie Dimon, TOM's pope on Wall Street, said when someone dared to suggest that a differential of more than ten thousand to one between high and average earners was simply wrong and incomes should be capped? Poor Jamie was quite hurt and complained that that would amount to punishing success. TOM's people do have a strange tendency to self-pity.

What to do? I fancy that Orwell, whose dad was a trafficker and understood this kind of thing all too well, would have found the words, the parables, the unblinking honesty, the courage to show us a way out. Better reincarnate quick, Eric Blair, the world needs you like never before.

John Burdett

John Burdett was brought up in North London and attended Warwick University where he read English and American Literature. This left him largely unemployable until he re-trained as a barrister and went to work in Hong Kong. He made enough money there to retire early to write novels. To date he has published seven novels, including the best selling Bangkok series: *Bangkok 8, Bangkok Tattoo, Bangkok Haunts, The Godfather of Kathmandu,* and *Vulture Peak.*

Joe—2012

Mike Lawson

At the time I was asked to contribute to *The Orwell Brigade*, I happened to be reading Curt Gentry's biography of J. Edgar Hoover, and the juxtaposition of Orwell's fears and Hoover's behavior immediately caused three questions to occur to me. First, can you imagine what a man like Hoover could have done if he had had access to the technology that exists today? Second, is anyone so naïve as to believe that people like J. Edgar Hoover don't exist today? And third, is it really the government we have to fear?

Hoover was director of the Federal Bureau of Investigation from 1924 to 1972, and it is a fact, as Gentry validates in his book, that during this period he used his agents to illegally gather information to discredit, incriminate and blackmail American citizens—and not just ordinary citizens. One reason, maybe the primary reason, why Hoover remained in power for almost fifty years was that his secret files contained information he used to blackmail some American presidents, men like John F. Kennedy, who had numerous extramarital affairs. But the other startling thing about Hoover's long, corrupt reign is that so many politicians, people whom

American history depicts as "good guys"—people like Harry Truman—went along with Hoover's tactics not because he blackmailed them but because he was *useful* to them. Pragmatism took precedence over principle.

The other thing I was struck by was how one hyphenated word, "un-American," was used to provide a legal or quasi-legal basis for the things Hoover did. What I mean by this is that Hoover was allowed to investigate American citizens not because there was evidence that they were traitors, terrorists or criminals but instead because he simply considered them un-American. In Hoover's mind, holding a political philosophy he disagreed with, such as socialism or communism, belonging to a labor union, supporting racial equality or simply disagreeing with or publically embarrassing Hoover were all considered un-American activities. The other truly startling thing is that Hoover was given legitimacy for his actions when the United States Congress formed one of the most draconian bodies to ever exist: the House Un-American Activities Committee, which existed from 1938 to 1975.

If Hoover decided a person was a political threat or, in his mind, an enemy of the state, the first thing he did was create a file on the person and then used his agents to collect data on the person. Hoover wanted to know if the subject associated with radicals (like socialists or civil rights leaders), belonged to "un-American" organizations (like labor unions) or had ever made statements that could be considered treasonous. He seemed obsessed with the sex lives of people he considered un-American. His agents investigated to see if they'd had extramarital affairs, interracial affairs or, ironically, if they were homosexual. And in the 1950s to be friends with a communist was to be a communist, and there was nothing more un-American than being a communist.

It was not easy, however, for Hoover's agents to acquire this information. It took a lot of men and lot of man-hours. His agents had to follow subjects and keep them under surveillance for long periods of time to see what they did and whom they knew. They scoured paper files containing membership records for various organizations, such as the communist party. They steamed open letters—with the full cooperation of the US Postal Service. They interviewed the subject's friends—and enemies—to see what damaging gossip they might reveal. They broke into homes, sometimes with a warrant and sometimes not, and installed crude listening devices and tapped into phone lines. And in order for Hoover's men—he employed very few women—to be able to record conversations, the agents often had to be in close proximity to the subject, such as in an adjacent hotel room, and would use stenographers to document whatever was said.

Hoover may not have invented the phrase "knowledge is power," but he certainly understood it.

Now imagine if J. Edgar Hoover lived in 2012.

Today, cameras are everywhere—and "everywhere" is not hyperbole. There are cameras to catch folks running red lights, surveillance cameras owned by businesses to prevent crime, cameras in cell phones, cameras in laptops to allow people to hold face-to-face conversations online, and cameras installed by the government for the purpose of catching terrorists. Several American city police forces are now using Predator drones—a literal eye-in-the-sky—to aid in reducing crime.

In addition to cameras that provide—or can be hacked to provide—a visual record of a person's activities, GPS microchips are installed in cell phones and automobiles. LoJack is your friend. If your car breaks down, the tow truck guy can find you; if your car is stolen, the cops can find it. At the same time, if an entity—private or public—wants to know where you are and where you've been, it's just a matter of accessing that little microchip in your cell phone.

Which leads to the way we communicate these days. Back in Hoover's day you had letters, the telegraph and multi-party telephone systems. As everyone knows, we've gone *way* beyond a telephone connected by a wire to another telephone. We have cell phones, which are basically radios; we email, text and use Skype, Facebook and Twitter. So these days it's a little more complicated than attaching a couple of alligator clips to a phone line as poor J. Edgar was required to do to monitor communications back in the 1950s. In fact, I based my sixth novel, *House Divided*, on this subject—specifically, the way that George W. Bush and the National Security Agency illegally monitored the communications of American citizens following 9/11.

The National Security Agency is America's largest intelligence service in terms of both personnel and funding. Its primary mission is eavesdropping. And eavesdropping, as practiced by the NSA, is not a man with his ear pressed to the wall. Eavesdropping means capturing *any* communication in *any* medium. Buried fiber-optic cables are tapped; microwave, radio and telephone transmissions are intercepted; satellites listen; codes are broken. No communication is *technically* safe from the NSA—but there is a small legal hurdle they are forced to overcome: a pesky law called FISA, the Foreign Intelligence Surveillance Act.

The father of FISA was the late Edward M. Kennedy, and he introduced his legislation following years of Senate investigations into Richard Nixon's use of domestic intelligence agencies (i.e., Hoover's boys) to spy on political activists. Surprisingly—or maybe not—Democrats *and* Republicans supported Ted's bill, including folks like Republican Strom Thurmond, a man not known for leaning far to the left. It appeared that neither conservatives nor liberals liked the idea of presidents ignoring the privacy protections guaranteed Americans by the Fourth Amendment.

FISA strictly prohibits *randomly* monitoring the communications of US citizens. That is, it does not allow an intelligence agency like the NSA or the FBI to listen to as many phone calls as it possibly can just hoping to hear two guys talking who might be terrorists. FISA says that if the spies want to eavesdrop on the communications of Americans, they need a warrant, and to get said warrant, the government has to be able to show that the persons of interest are suspected of being engaged in terrorism or espionage.

Getting these warrants isn't particularly difficult, however. The warrants are granted by the Foreign Intelligence Surveillance Court, a group of federal judges who act in total secrecy and whose decisions are not really monitored by anyone. Furthermore, *suspected* isn't a particularly challenging legal standard to meet. Nonetheless, obtaining these warrants takes time—and in the war on terror, minutes count—but more importantly, there is an obvious Catch-22. You might suspect that an American named Mohammed who attends a mosque led by a radical, fire-breathing, anti-American imam is plotting nefarious things, but you can't really be sure until you've listened to a few of Mohammed's calls. In other words, just being named Mohammed isn't sufficient justification for a warrant. (Not yet, anyway.)

So, you might conclude that FISA and the Fourth Amendment to the US Constitution can prevent an agency like the NSA with powerful technical capabilities from illegally eavesdropping on the conversations of private citizens—and you'd be wrong.

Along comes George W. Bush. Following 9/11, the President concluded that FISA was a major roadblock to his forces engaged in the War on Terror, and he issued an executive order which was never made public—really, it never was—which said that the NSA no longer needed a warrant to eavesdrop on folks suspected of terrorism. The President's intention, however, was never to spy on Americans communicating with other Americans. His intention was that if an American or a foreigner on American soil was a suspected terrorist and was calling *overseas*, then no warrant was required as it had been in the past. And to calm the nerves of those people at the NSA who were worried about going to jail for breaking the FISA laws, the President sent them to his top lawyer, the Attorney General. The AG told the spies not to worry, that the President's executive order trumped the law—and the NSA was off to the races.

The NSA did have one small problem, however: it's relatively easy to capture wireless signals—signals that swim through the atmosphere like blind fish, bouncing from tower to tower. The problem was that in the twenty-first century, the majority of all communications—voice and email—are routed through fiber-optic cables, and to tap into fiber-optic cables, the NSA needed to get into communication company switching stations and connect complex equipment and sophisticated computers to the cables. This meant that they needed the cooperation of the communication companies—companies like Verizon and

AT&T—and these companies agreed to cooperate, thanks in large part to the Justice Department's interpretation of the President's executive order. And once this equipment was installed, no matter what the President intended, it became possible to monitor *everyone's* communications.

It was impossible to listen to everything, of course. Every twelve-year-old in America, and maybe in the world, has a cell phone, and billions of calls, emails and text messages pass through fiber-optic cables every day. So the NSA's marvelous computers listened for key words and phrases, or calls going to certain locations, or calls spoken in certain languages. To use a simple example— the actual process is much more complicated—if a man in Washington speaking in Arabic said the words "white house" and "ka-boom" in the same sentence ... well, the spies at Fort Meade perked right up.

The NSA's warrantless eavesdropping program was a secret being kept by politicians, several thousand spies, telecommunications company employees, and big-mouthed lawyers at the Department of Justice, so it was no wonder that these illegal activities were eventually outed. The amazing thing is that the secret was kept for as long as it was, nearly four years, but in 2005 James Risen of the *New York Times* broke the story and things came to halt, and the NSA began to follow the rules again, meaning that they began seeking warrants again to eavesdrop. Or so they say.

Thus the technology exists to monitor virtually all communications, and it no longer requires teams of agents listening in on a wiretap and a stenographer jotting down conversations in Gregg shorthand. A few computers will now do all the work. There are, of course, encryption programs to prevent eavesdropping, but did I mention what the NSA's second job is? Their first job is eavesdropping. Their second job is breaking codes—i.e., encryption systems to prevent eavesdropping.

Then we come to the topic of information acquisition in general. Over the years people have periodically become concerned that law enforcement agencies such as the FBI might be given the authority to monitor library records. That is, the FBI would be allowed to see if you've checked out books related to developing nuclear, biological or chemical weapons, or if you've been reading the manifestos of sinister organizations advocating the overthrow of democracy. These days it seems almost laughable to be concerned about the government monitoring the books you check out from your local library. Why would you use a library when you have access to the Internet?

Today virtually all records are stored in computers. Who still has paper files? Also today, more often than not, people use credit cards to pay for things. Therefore, it's not really hard at all for someone who has the means and desire to do so, to figure out exactly what you own, what you read, what organizations you belong to, who you donate to, what medical problems you have, what drugs you take, etc. And I'm not talking about some B-movie nerd hacking into computer systems to gain access information—all you need is the cooperation of the fine folk who work for Google, Amazon, Facebook, banks, and communication and credit card companies. Now I realize, of course, that privacy laws supposedly protect this information, but it's not a matter of law.

The point is, the technology to collect information on citizens, to spy on folks from the sky, to monitor everyone's communications exists, and if a technology exists, it will be used. You can't un-ring the bell. And, as demonstrated by the NSA's warrantless eavesdropping program following 9/11, the law is no guarantee that people's privacy will be protected. All it takes is one powerful, motivated politician, like a J. Edgar Hoover or a George W. Bush, acting in secrecy, abetted by the private sector, and privacy as we know it ceases to exist.

But is it the government that people should really fear? Is the government George Orwell's fearsome Big Brother? I don't think so. Or at least I think the government is more likely to be the tool of the same people who buy our politicians and pay staggering amounts of money to ensure that laws are not passed to prevent them from doing the things they currently do.

It's the corporate sector that I fear, and those billionaires who run the corporate sector, who control our politicians. The power of lobbyists far outweighs the power of "one man, one vote." I often joke—though I'm not really joking—that America has the best government money can buy. And these corporations are not really American corporations; they are multinational companies that owe their allegiance only to the bottom line on a balance sheet, and not to any particular nation or political ideology.

Therefore I believe the greatest threat to privacy is corporate entities that can develop, and most likely already have developed, their own intelligence organizations. In fact, one recent event shows this to be true: Rupert Murdock's newspaper in England that was caught wiretapping and hacking into the computers of British politicians and celebrities to acquire information. What is also truly ironic about that case—and truly depressing—is that historically it was the "free press" that protected us from abuses of power. Today you have to be somewhat naive to believe that the press is truly autonomous when a few large corporations control newspapers and television companies.

Joe. 2012. Joe's a good guy. He decides he wants to run for office to cure the ills of society, to fight for the people, to right the wrongs he sees all about him. It doesn't really matter what political party Joe belongs to; he could be a Republican or a Democrat. So Joe runs for office, and it appears that he has a chance to win. He may become the next mayor of his city, the next congressman from his home state.

Then Joe makes a tragic error. He decides to take on an issue—and just like Joe's political party, the issue itself isn't really important. The only thing that is important is that the issue will negatively affect the profits of some corporation or the aspirations of some politician already owned by that corporation.

Joe now becomes a person of interest—and it doesn't take all that much to get a handle on Joe.

Joe takes antidepressant medication. This information is in his health-care provider's computers. Joe's daughter, per her medical records, had an abortion when she was sixteen. Joe's tax returns, filed online, show that in 2010 he didn't properly report some business expenses. (Joe claims his accountant made the error.) Joe traveled to Hawaii on a business trip and Joe's wife didn't go with him; his attractive, twenty-eight-year-old secretary occupied the seat next to him on the plane. Video footage from hotel security tapes shows Joe standing close—intimately close?—to his secretary in the lobby of Joe's hotel. Hotel records show the secretary didn't have her own room at the hotel. (She *said* she stayed with an old college roommate.) A text message sent by Joe to his secretary said, "Last night was great!" Joe meant the dinner he and his secretary attended with sixty other people. Or did he?

Joe's hotel bill shows he watched a pornographic movie—with or without his secretary isn't clear. His hotel bill also includes a minibar charge for six little bottles of vodka, all the liquor charged on the same night. It's not known whether Joe drank all those little bottles by himself or whether, as he later claimed, he and three men he was entertaining consumed the booze.

GPS records for Joe's rental car show that he parked directly across the street from a massage parlor that is a known house of prostitution. In fact, a security camera in a nearby store shows Joe crossing the street, heading directly toward the door of the massage parlor, and a woman who certainly looks like a hooker is waving to Joe. (Joe claims—but why would you take Joe's word over a camera's?—that he was actually headed to the drugstore next to the massage parlor.)

We now have a pretty good picture of Joe: a man who obviously supports abortion contrary to his stated pro-life position; a man who cheats on his taxes; a man who watches pornography, drinks too much and may be mentally unstable as evidenced by his medications; a man who probably—almost certainly—cheats on his wife. Now this doesn't mean that Joe won't be elected. In fact, he almost certainly will be elected because when Joe is presented with his "file," don't you think Joe will have a much better understanding of how he should vote on a certain issue?

Mike Lawson

Mike Lawson has published seven thrillers: *The Inside Ring*, *House Secrets*, and *House Divided* were all nominated for the Barry Award. *House Rules* was a Nancy Pearl Pick and an Indie Pick. *House Justice* was called "a perfect political thriller" by Library Journal. His seventh novel, *House Blood*, was released in July 2012 and Mike was recently featured on the Crime in the City series on the National Public Radio. Prior to turning to writing full time, Mike was a nuclear engineer employed by the Navy. He lives in the Northwest of the United States. For more information on Mike and his books go to www.mikelawsonbooks.com.

The Boulevard of Dreams and Nightmares: When Rich and Poor Live on the Same Street

John Lantigua

Your starting point is the Island of Palm Beach, a place synonymous with wealth.

Specifically, you begin your journey at the eastern end of a thoroughfare known as Southern Boulevard. That situates you a few yards from the Atlantic Ocean and also right outside Donald Trump's Mar-a-Lago, one of the country's poshest private clubs. The 126-room mansion was constructed in the 1920s by Marjorie Merriweather Post, the cereal heiress, who was married to E.J. Hutton, the renowned stockbroker. It was billed as the grandest private home ever built. Trump bought it in 1985 and transformed it into a watering hole for the rich and famous. Michael Jackson and Lisa Marie Presley spent their honeymoon there in 1994. It looks like a dwelling out of a fairy tale.

If you climb into your car and drive west 38.8 miles on that very same road, you reach Belle Glade, a majority black city on the banks of Lake Okeechobee that suffers some of the worst poverty in the country. Without using your turn signal even once, you go from a 20,000-square-foot Louis XIV ballroom, gilded ceilings and a $100,000 fee just to join Trump's club, to overflowing soup kitchens, a forty percent unemployment rate, child poverty at twice the national number, and people capturing rain in buckets because they can't afford to pay water bills.

Just go straight and you travel from opulence to profound privation. You can't get lost.

In 2011 the Census Bureau announced that poverty in the US had spread to forty-six million people and that the gap between the wealthiest and the poorest continued to grow. This was not news for a person like me. I write for a newspaper in Palm Beach County, Florida. I have driven Southern Boulevard. But it continues to amaze me how little the issue of wealth distribution seems to matter to most Americans. I find myself wondering how on earth we can expect to maintain a democracy when people lead existences that are so radically different from one another that we no longer seem to belong to the same species.

This take on class differences may sound radical to some. That may be because I have a frame of reference that differs from that of most Americans. I worked as a foreign correspondent in Latin America for years. I covered brutal civil wars in places like El Salvador and Guatemala, where entire rural villages were wiped out by army units because the poor people in those villages were thought to sympathize with leftist guerrillas. Men, women and children were slaughtered by the hundreds. The occasional guilt-ridden soldier emerged later to tell grisly tales—babies skewered on bayonets. The armies were doing the bidding of the well-to-do in those countries in the name of anti-communism. I realized that people can only treat each other that way when they no longer see each other as belonging to the same human race, the same species. That is what enormous differences between haves and have-nots can do to a society.

Of course, we are speaking about the US, not rural El Salvador. But that doesn't mean that lives aren't being lost in the war that we are experiencing here. Lately, we hear certain politicians accusing anyone who criticizes income distribution in the US of trying to ignite a class war in this country. The fact is that class war has been going on a long time, except only one side has been fighting.

Since long before the Great Recession, economists have documented the skewing of wealth in the US. By 2007, just before the economic downturn, twenty-three percent of all income earned in the US went into the pockets of the top one percent of richest Americans. The country had not reached that degree of income inequality since 1928, the year before the Great Depression when thirty-eight percent of all wealth—net assets—had seeped into the same few pockets. Can that possibly be good for democracy?

After I began to plan this essay, but before I sat down to write it, I was assigned to cover a murder for my newspaper. A forty-nine-year-old white man, Jimmy McMillan, whose family had run a grocery store in a black neighborhood in Belle Glade for fifty years, and who himself had an excellent relationship with his black customers, was gunned down by a would-be robber behind his store counter early on the morning of January 2.

As I drove out there just a couple of hours later, I turned onto Southern Boulevard not far from Trump's Mar-a-Lago and headed for Belle Glade. As I drove west, I passed through a number of towns and a variety of middle-class neighborhoods—from lower middle-class enclaves of smaller cottages to gated communities occupied by residents who had done better, though not as well as the gentry on the Island of Palm Beach.

All those middle-class inhabitants had a couple of things in common. First, their homes were worth much less than they had been five years before, due to the bursting of the housing bubble. Some former residents had lost their homes altogether because of mortgage schemes that had made a number of individuals very wealthy.

The other thing those middle-class families had in common was that their incomes were all worth less than they had been thirty years before. Whereas the wealthy had seen their share of the country's assets rise in recent decades, the middle class had seen its share of the pie eaten away. Many people now owed more on their houses than the houses were worth. They had no net assets. So I was driving from the wealth on the eastern end of the county to the poverty found on the western boundary and passing through what was supposed to be the middle ground. But that middle territory had been transformed into a landscape of shrunken prospects, increased struggle and pockets of despair.

Jimmy McMillan, who had been shot to death, was one of those who had belonged to the middle class.

On the morning of his death a surveillance camera caught the entire crime. The shooter wore a gray bandana over his face but nonetheless was soon identified. His name was Corey Graham, a nineteen-year-old local black who until the year before had played for Glades Central High School's storied football program. The school has won state championships and sent countless players to top football colleges across the nation and about twenty players to the National Football League. Football has been for many local young black men the way out of a dead-end future.

At six feet two and 280 pounds, Graham had played offensive line and been named a first team all-star in his region. He was also a B-minus student, with nothing more serious than a traffic ticket on his police record. But somehow he had fallen through the cracks between the college football recruiters. Ironically, one coach said Graham hadn't made it to a big-time college football program because he just wasn't mean enough.

As I finished the forty-mile drive, the last twenty miles or so through vast fields of sugar cane, I drove into town and saw what I had seen every time I had driven there over the previous ten years: decrepit buildings that should have been condemned but couldn't be because there was just nowhere else for people to live, and lots of unemployed young men sitting on porches or standing on streets in the middle of the day. About twenty years back the sugar industry mechanized, the thousands of cane cutters who once came to town disappeared, commerce dried up, and the local families were left standing on street corners. It is not difficult to find people in Belle Glade who have not had steady work in well over a decade. Town leaders have begged for investment—from the other side of the county and from anywhere else in the state and country—but have come up empty.

It emerged later that Graham had enrolled at a local community college but had also begun hanging out with some of those chronically unemployed young men and spending more and more time on the street. In high school he'd had the structure of a serious football program to shape his life. Now many of Graham's teammates were gone, away at college. Without them and his coaches, surrounded by hopelessness and a sense that he had missed the one train out of town, he went off the rails. Corey Graham killed Jimmy McMillan for a fistful of cash.

Jimmy McMillan, a middle-class man, had been caught in the middle, between Corey Graham's one lost chance at a rich future and the reality of poverty in his hometown. Jimmy might as well have been run over by a car speeding from Palm Beach Island to Belle Glade on Southern Boulevard, a thoroughfare that connects hope to despair in today's America.

I picked up the *New York Times* business section yesterday and read how much the CEOs of America's top investment banks took home last year. The leaders of JP Morgan Chase, Wells Fargo, Goldman Sachs, Citigroup, and Bank of America made anywhere from $8.1 million to $23 million. That is down from a few years ago.

Bruce Nissen, a nationally known expert on labor issues, based at Florida International University in Miami, and an acquaintance of mine, confirms that in Palm Beach County we are in the belly of the beast when it comes to the wealth gap. That is because the wealthy find Florida very accommodating. "There are advantages that bring them to Florida, starting with no state income tax and almost no unions, so they can find low-income service workers to work for them. You end up with a bifurcated society."

Bifurcated means branching off in two different directions. In Palm Beach County you find the two extremes on the opposite ends of one thoroughfare. The super-wealthy and the destitute live on the same street—the Boulevard of Dreams and Nightmares.

John Lantigua

John Lantigua shared the the Pulitzer Prize for Investigative Reporting in 1999 and the Robert Kennedy Journalism Prize in 2004 and 2006. He is the author of seven novels. *The Lady from Buenos Aires* (2007) and *On Hallowed Ground* (2011) both won the International Latino Book Award for Mystery Writing.

Wading While Black: Suspects in Fact and Crime Fiction

Gary Phillips

When images of the devastation wrought by Hurricane Katrina filled American television screens in August 2005, I recall vividly an overhead shot of a black man and woman wading in damn near chest-high water. The woman was holding some food items, as was the man. The two were termed looters. The Associated Press ran a similar photo of a young black man in high water, stating he'd recently looted a grocery store. During that same time the Agence France-Presse (AFP) ran a photo of a white man and woman wading in water with food items, and they were captioned as finding bread and soda.

While such obviously racist characterizations of black folk people scrambling for survival like their fellow white citizens of New Orleans were immediately lambasted in various circles, that labeling symbolized decades, centuries even, of the kind of loaded depictions black people and other people of color have endured in the mass media in America. For instance, recently on National Public Radio's *Fresh Air* program—transcribed on theroot.com, a black-centric website—*Girls* creator Lena Dunham addressed the issue of the all-white cast of central characters on her episodic show on HBO, a cable network: "I wrote the first season primarily by myself, and I co-wrote a few episodes. But I am a half-Jew, half-WASP, and I wrote two Jews and two WASPs. Something I wanted to avoid was tokenism in casting. If I had one of the four girls, if, for example, she was African-American, I feel like—not that experience of an African-American girl and a white girl are drastically different, but there has to be specificity to that experience [that] I wasn't able to speak to."

I applaud Dunham's candor, but hers is an old refrain the suits in Hollywood have parroted for decades as well. Movies or television shows with black leads don't do well in the international market, they say. Or the reason a particular movie or TV show fails domestically if there's a black lead (and if there is a black lead, you can bet his or her buddy is white) is that it didn't have "universal" appeal—a code word for white. Mind you, this could be a character who is a doctor, a lawyer or a cop—still the three staples of television fare—a character who comes to the aid of all sorts of people in all sorts of situations. Or the character could be a handsome, *clever* spy.

As I wrote in a piece called "Race and Ratings" for the online site FourStory back in 2011, the annals of pop culture will little note *nor* long remember the passing of the NBC network show *Undercovers*. This was an effort about Steven and Samantha Bloom (played by the photogenic Boris Kodjoe and Gugu Mbatha-Raw), who ran a tony catering service and just happened to be retired CIA operatives—I suppose the idea here being they got to sample all sorts of cuisine in various locales while carrying out their assassinations and retrieval missions.

The setup of *Undercovers* demanded that their old life would pull them back into its orbit. It was a breezy and frothy show, where the Blooms might dash off to North Korea supposedly to work for a humanitarian agency but really to retrieve the flux capacitor prototype or some such. The handsome couple would engage in witty banter as they did their derring-do, dodging bullets and kung fu'ing the shit out of the bad guys along the way.

The series wasn't anything we hadn't seen before in the subgenre of fast and furious, fun-loving spies and their shenanigans. *Undercovers* particularly drew from the 1980s TV show *Scarecrow and Mrs. King* and the twenty-first-century big-budget actioner *Mr. and Mrs. Smith*. In the former the initial setup was that this spy, nicknamed Scarecrow, involves an ordinary middle-class hausfrau in his various espionage outings, and in the latter a married couple each do black ops work unbeknownst to the other. What was different in *Undercovers*, its double entendre tagline being "Sexpionage," was that the two leads, the Blooms, were black. As I'd noted in the FourStory piece, I couldn't recall then or now another network television offering where that had been the case. On HBO, a pay cable service, there had been *The Wire*, the engaging crime drama set in the drug world of Baltimore. It was a show with a large black cast of cops, criminals and pols along with their white counterparts. But given its hardcore nature—not to overlook its critique of capitalism—*The Wire* was a layered narrative that couldn't play out on the network stage.

By its fourth year, despite being lauded by critics and having crime fiction readers and writers as fans, *The Wire* had average ratings of 1.6 million households, dismal by network standards. Yet *The Wire* would go on to be renewed for a fifth and final season and has, rightly, gained near-legendary status. *Undercovers* dropped from 8.57 million viewers for its premiere (which even today with a fragmented viewing audience isn't a good number for a network show) to 5.45 million by its October 27 airing. It was canceled soon thereafter.

Why my fascination with an otherwise forgettable effort like *Undercovers*? Because in the timeline between the AP's looter caption to the 2008 election of the first black president of the United States to now, it did not signal an era of color-blindness as some had hoped. Notwithstanding apt criticism of Obama's policies, how deep, how engrained is the American form of racism, that gun sales, neo-Nazi groups and bizarre conspiracy theories have flourished in the wake of his coming to office?

Are these people who only listen to right-wing blowhard Rush Limbaugh on the radio and only watch channels that rerun shows from the '50s and '60s ... fitting their notion of when black folk were invisible to them, and America was white and all right? Granted that the scripts for *Undercovers* weren't exactly Emmy caliber, but when has that ever stopped a TV show from succeeding? The Blooms as played by Mbatha-Raw and Kodjoe were dashing, had chemistry and were clearly relatable as goes the Hollywood term. Their race wasn't a factor in the plots, and I'd wager their roles were originally envisioned for white leads. Tellingly, though, when notice of the show's demise was known, this reader comment was posted on the Deadline: Hollywood site:

> Okay so nobody wants to bring up the big flaw in the premise because it would be too un-PC—so I will have a go—the point of being an undercover spy is to infiltrate some level of a society or a bureaucracy to take care of business. And if you are really a US spy that probably means blending into somewhere in Eastern or Western Europe, Asia, maybe Latin America. And there have to

be pretty limited ways where Black/African American spies won't stick out physically from the people around them. There can only be so many contrived ways to put them on the scene where it wouldn't be important for them to "blend" and soon you are starting to bore or aggravate your audience. [This comment is attributed to Mariah D.]

That's sounds like an easy argument to make [says FunkDubious in response] but it's actually just facile. Because white people have a hard time conceiving of non-whites in places and positions that don't fit their own internal narrative they deem such depictions as unrealistic. A family friend was an Army Intelligence officer stationed in Italy during WWII. There were black Marines on Pelelu. But to look at anything from *Private Ryan* to the otherwise excellent BoB [*Band of Brothers*] and the Pacific all the way back to *Rat Patrol* you'd think black people weren't allowed to leave America before 1939.

Here we are in a time when technology has delivered Google's road tests of its driverless robot cars, endless entertainment platforms and outlets, and a plethora of data that used to require physical research at the library, all available by a few strokes on a keypad, yet too often the perception of who and what black people are is still framed by long-held, outdated, patronizing notions that might as well have sprung from the pages of *Gone with the Wind*. Though maybe that's to be expected when you have an anti-intellectual backlash fueled by right-wing forces, where a good percentage of people actually believe the Earth is only 6,000 years old and that we lived like the Flintstones back then—humans and dinosaurs existing together.

Then too, as documented by a recent report by the New York City American Civil Liberties Union, NYPD officers "stopped and frisked" 685,724 times in 2011. Young black and Latino men were the targets of a hugely disproportionate number of these stops. For although they account for only 4.7 percent of the city's population, black and Latino males between the ages of fourteen and twenty-four accounted for 41.6 percent of those stops. The number of stops of young black men exceeded the entire city population of young black men (168,126 as compared to 158,406). Ninety percent of young black and Latino men stopped were innocent.

Is it any wonder, then, in the wake of the killing of teenager Trayvon Martin by self-appointed, one-man community-watch wannabe cop George Zimmerman, you have somebody like Geraldo Rivera on Fixed—that is, Fox—News, stating that the young man was as much to blame as Zimmerman for his death because of *what he was wearing*? "But I am urging the parents of black and Latino youngsters particularly to not let their children go out wearing hoodies," Rivera would state subsequently on Fox.

Why of course Zimmerman must have thought this slightly built kid was up to no good, daring to walk along a street like any other person with his bag of Skittles candy and can of iced tea because he "fit the profile"— young, black and male. Maybe Zimmerman spent too much time watching episodes of *The Wire* back to back on DVD and concluded only slangers wore hoodies. Don't all those gangsta rappers with their nines tucked into their waistbands and their handkerchiefs declaring their colors hanging out of their back pockets be decked out in them hoodies?

While Rivera would backtrack, recast his words amid the resulting outcry over his comments, I have to be honest and admit that some of how he advised his own dark-hued son to not be walking around with his pants hanging low or in a hoodie are pretty much words my wife and I said to our son. Miles is twenty-five now, but as a tall and muscular teen who was a baller, a basketball player, we were keenly aware of how police, gangbangers and others would perceive this young black man in our racially mixed neighborhood. What with his baritone voice, Miles perfectly fit certain perceptions, and he and his friends getting routinely stopped by the cops confirmed this for us.

Our son was born a year before *Straight Outta Compton* dropped in 1988. While this was not the first gangsta rap album, this seminal work by N.W.A., Niggaz Wit Attitudes, was a breakout, a crossover hit—it made money. The album also got the media's attention and signaled rap was an art form the music business couldn't ignore. While the album is not a call to arms as much as it glorifies dope slangin', drinking forties (forty-ounce bottles of malt liquor), and bedding as many woman as you can stand, one of its numbers became an incendiary audio touchstone, vocalizing a long-held sentiment in many parts of the black and brown inner city. "Comin straight from the underground/Young nigga got it bad cuz I'm brown/And not the other color so police think/ They have the authority to kill a minority ..." went the opening lines of the battle cry "Fuck tha Police." In the days of rage that consumed Los Angeles post the not-guilty verdicts of the four cops in the Rodney King beating that April and May of 1992, "Fuck tha Police" became socio-political graffiti spray-painted on various walls.

Before that song came along, community organizations like the Coalition Against Police Abuse (CAPA, where I received my political-organizing baptism of fire) had been doing demonstrations and speak-outs over various outrageous incidents involving the Los Angeles Police Department, the LAPD. We'd been galvanized by incidents such as when Eulia Love, a widow and single mother in South Central who owed $22.09 on her overdue gas bill, wound up being slain by two cops, one black and one white, after she got into an altercation with the meter man from the gas company who'd come to her home to collect or turn off the gas.

Or take the incendiary words of then-police chief Daryl Gates. This was in an interview with the *L.A. Times*, a newspaper he considered liberal and biased against him and the Department. The context was there had been an outcry by segments of the public as to why a disproportionate number of black male suspects had died while in custody after the chokehold was applied on them. This was a compliance measure, to use the police euphemism. The nightstick would be applied against the carotid artery in the neck, in this way shutting down blood flow to the brain. Often the police would say the suspect was high on PCP, angel dust, and therefore hard to control. But as that catchall excuse got to be tiresome, Gates stated in the article: "We may be finding that in some blacks when [the chokehold] is applied, the veins or arteries do not open up as fast as they do in normal people."

To say the least, Gates was a polarizing figure in his tenure as chief. In Operation Hammer, he masterminded a massive sweep of supposed gangbangers, scooping up black and brown young men "for anything and everything," as Joe Domanick recalled an officer telling him during the roundup in his well-done Edgar Award-winning book about the history of the Department, *To Protect and to Serve: The LAPD's Century of War in the City of Dreams*. It was like something out of a film about a coup by Gillo Pontecorvo, the director of *The Battle of Algiers*. Youth were herded at night onto the grassy field of the Coliseum, an open-air pro sports venue next door to the University of Southern California in South Central … or as private college USC would say, they are downtown adjacent. LAPD officers sat at portable tables *booking* their arrestees under the floodlights. The youths were then taken away in paddy wagons while helicopters—Ghetto Birds as the rappers called them—circled overhead.

An iconic and ironic image of this period was First Lady Nancy Reagan going along with Gates and his CRASH officers—Community Resources Against Street Hoodlums—as they conducted raids on alleged drug houses or in search of suspects in South Central. In keeping with the state of siege theme, the "batter ram" was often the method of door knock Gates employed on these excursions. This was a military-style armored vehicle outfitted with a battering ram, a steel pole essentially, used to cave in security screen doors and windows, and sometimes the side of a house. There's a TV clip of the First Lady getting her makeup right for the cameras sitting in one of these bad boys. DJ Toddy Tee would release on homemade cassette tape his sardonic sendup of this Gatesian method of entry in his song, "Batterram." He imposed new lyrics over the song "Rappin' Duke," Jeff Chang notes in his book *Can't Stop Won't Stop: A History of the Hip-Hop Generation*. "Batterram" became an underground hit.

The song got luv again recently during the twentieth anniversary of the '92 riots—or civil unrest, depending on your point of view. Those events were recalled by those in it or on its periphery in Los Angeles. To be sure, it wasn't just the cops getting exonerated in the criminal proceedings that caused the riots to be touched off at the intersection of Florence and Normandie in South Central that April 29, after the verdicts were announced a little past three in the afternoon.

On the morning of March 16, 1991—about two weeks after King's beating in the early morning hours of March 3, caught surreptitiously on video by George Holliday—fifteen-year-old high school student Latasha Harlins stopped in the Empire Liquor Market Deli on Figueroa near Manchester in the 'hood to buy a bottle of orange juice. She put the juice in her backpack, holding the money for the item as she came to the counter. The fifty-one-year-old Soon Ja Du, a Korean national behind the counter assumed the girl was trying to steal from her store and they got into a heated argument. Du grabbed at Latasha's backpack and the girl struck her. Latasha then threw the orange juice bottle on the counter and turned to leave, whereupon Du shot her in the back of the head, killing her instantly. Latasha's death was recorded on the store's video.

Ultimately, Judge Joyce Karlin would essentially exonerate Du, who was *convicted* of manslaughter but giving her probation and no jail time. Karlin would soon face a recall that failed, and years later she would go on to serve on the city council of Manhattan Beach (a small enclave in what is called the South Bay, near LA) for two terms—and the Empire was firebombed during the unrest.

As I'd noted on a radio show and in print during the anniversary, those events inspired me to write what would become my first mystery novel, *Violent Spring*. At the time of the conflagration I was the outreach director for the Liberty Hill Foundation, an entity that today still funds community organizing, particularly in the hard-hit parts of town where the rioting occurred. I grew up in South Central, and my background included being a community organizer on a variety of issues including police abuse, Central American solidarity, and renters' rights. On the second day of the civil unrest, my wife took our young kids in the family van to the Valley to stay with friends out there and subsequently a cabin in the country. I stayed at our house in Mid-City—smoke in the air—armed with my .357 and courage out of a bottle of Jack Daniel's. But I was thinking these events could be a hell of a plot for a book.

By 1994 I had become one of the directors of the MultiCultural Collaborative (there were three of us, a modern Mod Squad, a politically correct troika: one black, one Korean-American, one Chicano), founded a few months post the riots to better race relations at the grass roots and affect public policy, and *Violent Spring* became my first published novel. Not only had I drawn on my past experiences, but my current work took me from the housing projects in Watts, meeting with gangbangers about the gang truce, to the high-rises of downtown and soirées in Beverly Hills. This gave me my settings, and interacting with the personalities would give me the composite characters for the book. This would be the landscape that my rough and tumble black private eye, Ivan Monk, would navigate in the murder that sets the story in motion. *Violent Spring,* set roughly a year or so after the unrest, begins at a groundbreaking for a shopping center at Florence and Normandie.

Also dropping during that heightened time post the unrest was Ice-T's "Cop Killer" song (written by Ernie

C), from the *Body Count* album, in which Gates and Rodney King got name-checked: "I got my twelve gauge sawed off/I got my headlights turned off/I'm 'bout to bust some shots off/I'm 'bout to dust some cops off." President Bush the First and future Second Lady Tipper Gore lambasted its lyrics, though they and other critics didn't address how those sentiments about the police had arisen in people of color communities. The most surreal moment of the backlash had to be the public reading conservative actor Charlton Heston did in an effort to embarrass Time-Warner at a shareholder's meeting about dropping Ice-T from its label. In his Moses-like stentorian tones he recited from "Cop Killer" and "KKK Bitch," another song on the album. If only Ice-T could have gotten Heston to do a duet with him for charity.

While *Violent Spring* grew out of Sa-i-Gu, the Korean term for the '92 riots, the book was actually building on a sort of third wave of black crime and mystery writing that had begun with Gar Anthony Haywood's 1988 award-winning novel *Fear of the Dark*, introducing his private eye character Aaron Gunner. This brace of writers would offer fresh takes in a genre long dominated by white perspectives.

"It was one of the mixed blocks over on Central Avenue, the blocks that are not yet all Negro." So muses Raymond Chandler's Philip Marlowe in the opening line of *Farewell, My Lovely,* published in 1940. In the retro *Devil in a Blue Dress* by Walter Mosley, published in 1990 but set in LA after World War II, his reluctant private eye Easy Rawlins notes in the beginning, "I was surprised to see a white man walk into Joppy's bar." And in Haywood's book, set in the modern era and told in third person, "The white boy with the funny left eye walked into the Acey Deuce on a Monday Night Football night."

Where the white Marlowe is merely passing through the black part of town in search of an errant husband, black Rawlins and Gunner are denizens of the Watts and South Central areas. In the time period of *Devil*, Los Angeles is officially segregated by housing covenants whose restrictions are enforced by the courts and the police. *Fear*'s era was when Gates was police chief. Early in his career he'd been a driver for police chief William Parker. This man openly sought to keep the "natives" contained in the jungle by running newspaper advertisements for white men to come from the segregated '50s and '60s South to join the LAPD.

When the Watts Riot exploded in August of '65 after, as the saying goes, a routine traffic stop of Marquette Frye by the Highway Patrol, a racist, clueless Parker, unable and unwilling to see black folk as citizens too, would expound, "It is estimated that by 1970, forty-five percent of the metropolitan area of Los Angeles will be Negro," Domanick relates in his book. "If you want any protection for your home ... you're going to have to get in *and* support a strong police department. If you don't, come 1970, God help you."

The initial wave of black mystery and crime writers is often traced as arising out of the Harlem Renaissance when Dr. Rudolph Fisher published what is considered the first black urban mystery novel, *The Conjure-Man Dies*. The book featured his black protagonists Dr. John Archer and plainclothesman Perry Dart. A play was crafted from the book and starred musician-actor Arthur "Dooley" Wilson (immortalized as Sam the piano player in *Casablanca*) as a singing detective. As Frankie Bailey notes in her well-researched book, *Out of the Woodpile: Black Characters in Crime and Detective Fiction*, Fisher would die at the young age of thirty-seven after being operated on for an intestinal ailment. He'd written other types of work but had also done a mystery short story with Archer and Dart called "John Archer's Nose."

Before Fisher there was Walter Adolphe Roberts, a Jamaican-born writer who penned various mystery stories including the 1926 novel *The Haunting Hand*—though in this book all the main characters are white. Writer and organizer Alice Dunbar-Nelson's short story "Summer Session" was written about the same time as Fisher's book in 1932. It was republished in 1995 in *Spooks, Spies and Private Eyes: Black Mystery, Crime and Suspense Fiction of the 20th Century*, edited by Paula Woods, who authored the Charlotte Justice series. That story was reprinted in 2009 in *Black Noir: Mystery Crime and Suspense Fiction by African-American Writers*, edited by Otto Penzler, which also reprinted "On Saturday the Siren Sounds at Noon," a '40s-era work by Ann Petry, also first republished in *Spooks, Spies*.

George S. Schyler, an African American socialist turned conservative, had a black plainclothes detective in his 1933 short story, "The Shoemaker Murder." A few years later he would serialize in the black *Pittsburgh Courier* newspaper from 1936 to '38 what became the pulp thriller *Black Empire*. In it journalist Carl Slater tangles with Dr. Belsidus and his organization, the Black Internationale. Belsidus seeks to achieve worldwide pan-Africanism and crush the white colonial powers.

Much more down to earth was Clarence Cooper Jr.'s *The Scene* (1960, Crown/Random House), part of the second wave: "All the elements of the Scene—the lights, the whores, the tricks in their cars, the razzle of jazz music from the record shop on the corner of Seventy-Seventh and Maple—repelled Rudy, the pimp and pusher, made him feel alien, a person without stable ground or purpose, although he knew no other atmosphere but this." Like two other hardcore writers who would be published later in the '60s, Donald Goines and Robert Beck—the two erstwhile Godfathers of Ghetto Lit, also referred to as Street Lit or Urban Lit (Beck, aka Iceberg Slim, was a former pimp whose life and fiction would inspire gansgta rapper Tracy Morrow, aka Ice-T, to adopt his swagger and moniker)—Cooper wrote from hard-earned experience. He battled his own addiction to heroin off and on and died in 1978, alone and penniless, after OD'ing in a room at the 23rd Street YMCA in Manhattan.

Except for Chester Himes, who deservedly enjoys cult status for his Coffin Ed Johnson and Gravedigger Jones absurdist mystery novels, other African American writers in the field of crime and mystery such as Cooper, Vern E. Smith (*The Jones Men*), Robert Dean Pharr (*Givedamn Brown*), Herbert Simmons (*Corner Boy*), and Nathan Heard (*Howard Street* and *House of Slammers*) are old school writers that most white Americans, and for that matter, many black Americans, don't remember today—even though, for instance, Heard's *Howard Street* was a million seller.

K'wan, Vickie Stringer, Omar Tyree, and Noire, among many others, conversely, are Ghetto Lit writers known and read by a generation raised on hip hop and video games, and generally despised by the black literati represented by the likes of Terry McMillan (*Waiting to Exhale*). Her 2007 letter to specific editors at Simon & Schuster blasted the house for publishing "poorly written black oriented titles—novels that depict wall-to-wall crime, sex, violence and hip hop ghetto-fabulousness."

Like much of gangsta rap that today merely parodies itself—all about bling and getting over—much of Ghetto Lit is redundant and one-dimensional. *The Ski Mask Way, Hood Rat* and *Project Chick* will unlikely advance the canon of crime fiction by many degrees. But that's not to dismiss the subgenre out of hand because, like the hardboiled gritty works of Cornel Woolrich and Jim Thompson, whose stories were filled with reprehensible characters, there is room for black characters in that regard as well.

Like *Straight Outta Compton* signaling the rise of gangsta rap, *True to the Game* by Teri Woods marked the coming of Ghetto Lit. She initially self-published her crime novel in 1998, after being rejected by twenty publishers over a period of six years. By 1999 Woods was on the map after countless hours of hand-selling her book, hustling it at stalls she rented at swap meets and literally on the street. Vickie Stringer's *Let That Be the Reason* was also initially self-published in 2002, the same year *The Wire* debuted. Stringer is in the lineage of Iceberg Slim and Goines (who began writing his first book while in the joint, being inspired after reading Iceberg's *Pimp: The Story of My Life*—a fictionalized accounting). She too began writing her book while doing five years in the federal pen, for selling a kilo of cocaine to a snitch, a CI (confidential informant).

Again, just as *Straight Outta Compton* alerted the white record establishment that rap was a money-maker, Woods and Stringer, leading the way for many others, would have their books republished by New York-based white publishers when they saw the sort of sales they'd racked up to a niche of readers these publishers hadn't reached. Stringer and Woods would also maintain their own indie publishing labels as well. At one point rappers

Snoop Dog and 50 Cent had Ghetto Lit imprints with St. Martin's and Pocket Books, respectively. Today Cash Money Content, the publishing arm of the Cash Money rap record label and distributed by Atria, part of Simon & Schuster, has republished Iceberg Slim's *Pimp* and *Airtight Willie and Me*, about two conmen, one of whom looks white. McMillan's letter, it seems, didn't trump potential book sales.

I'm a consumer of pop culture and a purveyor of genre fiction. I write about good and bad characters, flawed men and women of various races and ethnicities. On one hand I like to think I don't adhere to hidebound dogma such as W.E.B. Du Bois's admonishment to Harlem Renaissance writers like Rudolph Fisher to portray black folk in the best light, highlighting the merits of the Talented Tenth in their work. Conversely, I'm aware of the historic and ongoing way in which people of color and black people in particular are portrayed in the media and how they are perceived. After all, a vile outfit calling itself the Hiller Armament Company of Virginia sold gun targets that looked like the silhouette of Trayvon Martin, complete with a hoodie, holding Skittles and a can of iced tea. Done supposedly to raise money for George Zimmerman's defense.

What I write still reflects the awe I felt as a kid when my aunt gave me a copy of *From the Twilight Zone*, short stories derived from Rod Serling's *Twilight Zone* teleplays. Having seen the reruns of the TV shows, I was amazed to read those episodes, get inside the characters' heads, learn what they were feeling, and experience in a whole new way through the prose. But the *Twilight Zone* in its science fiction and fantasy episodes dealt with intolerance, small-minded people and the joys of small hopes. That told me years later that even though I write genre fiction, realities of race, class, and the other dynamics of the human condition could be reflected in my stories too.

Let me close with a sardonically cautionary passage from "Why Black People Don't Buy Books" by the late Ralph Wiley. I had the pleasure to interview him once for a newspaper piece. He was a keen, tongue-in-cheek observer in the Jonathan Swift mold and is much missed. This is excerpted from his collection of essays, *What Black People Should Do Now: Dispatches from Near the Vanguard*. I keep the following in mind so my head doesn't get too big for my hats in the pursuit of this writing game.

> If I had been born one hundred years earlier, a bare sliver of time's difference, I could have been shot or hanged for reading a book, let alone for writing one and trying to get it published. I wonder if knowing this helps me avoid blocks and keeps me studying the locks and bars on the publishers' gates. I know that what I don't know is always too much.

Gary Phillips

Gary Phillips draws on his experiences ranging from printer, labor organizer, to delivering dog cages in writing his tales of chicanery and malfeasance. He is the co-editor and contributor to *Send My Love and a Molotov Cocktail*. His short story is included in the *Heroin Chronicles*, and his novel, *Warlord of Willow Ridge*, explores crime at the time of the Great Recession. Visit his website at: www.gdphillips.com.

One in Any Given Night

Ernesto Mallo

The nights are darker. The days are dark in spite of the sun. One speaks quietly or one does not speak at all. One suspects everyone and we are all suspects. The thugs dictate lessons about good and evil. An interrogation is just around the corner under the supervision of the blind eye of a gun or a rifle.

One thinks he shouldn't have stayed out so late. One had better know what to answer if asked about it. One shouldn't be nervous even though One can see the soldier's finger tremble, poised on the trigger of the gun pointed at his head. The Commandant looks at One and seems to think maybe he'll let One go home to his bed. One feels himself a despicable man as he looks around for someone who appears more a suspect than he is in the eyes of those who have imprisoned him. Yes, One is a captive until they decide otherwise. Ten steps back. One is free, or so he feels. The Commandant looks at One and seems to think, taps on his chin with One's identity card. One tries to banish from his mind the stories told of what they do to those who are taken to their chambers. One should avoid fear because the dogs of the regime can smell it and ask, examine, inquire: Why are you afraid? What makes you tremble like that? Our people are not afraid because they have a clean conscience. Huh? Answer me, answER ME, anSWER ME, ANSWER ME YOU FUCK.

One makes up a story. I caught a cold, this is a long winter, so I caught a cold, and the other suspect he seeks does not appear. Above the head of the Commandant, in a window, a still silhouette observes them. One knows what the silhouette is looking at, for he has observed the same scene from his window a thousand times before. And he was happy then not to be the One below, targeted, interrogated and shitting his pants in fear. The sad joy at the misfortune of others—shameful, unspeakable. Even joy is poisoned in a police state.

The Commandant looks at the document, looks at One, back to the document, back to One. The Commandant has a poker player's eyes, the eyes of a man who, having inflicted so much torment and murder on others, has ended up with a dead soul. One knows the guy is shit and has power over life and death. One fears that his eyes, which are not dead, are fires beaming with hatred that the Commandant has seen so many times in his victims. The beam that reveals One is actually his enemy. The Commandant makes a gesture with his tight mouth and his eyes give off a cold, dispassionate and curious anger.

One feels lost, but then it happens. One ceases to be the exclusive focus of the Commandant's attention. Turning the corner, a couple appear: they are young, cute and, what is worse, they are laughing. The Commandant turns to them fast and mechanically. Seeing the military, the kids try to continue their journey quietly, but an almost undetectable gesture of the Commandant to one of his soldiers stops them. She wears a flowered summer frock, too light for winter, and the boy's jacket over her shoulders. Unfortunately for her she is quite sexy. The boy is delicate, a shy moustache barely showing. They are split up, a soldier talking to the guy, the Commandant focusing on the girl. One feels the horrible relief of being no longer interesting.

The Commandant smiles at the girl and asks where she lives, who with, what does her father do for a living. What the Commandant really wants is to make sure she is not a relative of someone important. One does not hear what they say, but he can read the body language: she seems to get smaller by the minute; the Commandant seems to grow larger; the boy has been reduced to a stuttering child. They all seem to have forgotten One, alone and witnessing the Commandant devouring with his eyes the girl in the flowery summer frock too light for winter.

The Commandant has arrived at the conclusion that the girl is a nobody, just an ordinary girl ending her teen years. Then One clears his throat, loudly, to remind the others that he is still there. The Commandant turns to One with parsimonious impatience. He approaches One with an air of one who seeks a fight. The Commandant stops, his face is an inch from One's. He extends the identity card towards One. When One is about to take it, the Commandant drops it and remains staring at him. One bends down to pick it up. The Commandant's words sound like a threat: "Carry on."

The Commandant slowly turns, showing him his wide back, and making the point that he is armed. One look at the gun hanging from his belt. One wishes to take it from him and shoot him dead on the spot. But One can't; he does not know how, nor has he the courage. One puts in his pocket the card that says nothing about his true identity, turns and walks away.

One does not turn when he hears the engines roaring and the troops leaving with their prey between their teeth. He ups his pace to get home where, with a racing heart, One will try to seduce with dreams, lulled to sleep by the rattle of machine guns.

The Big Picture

War and dictatorship are both children of the same mother: greed. All wars and dictatorships are established in the name of God, but their real aim is money. This is their first and ultimate reason. What dictators want is to be rich. Never in history has there been a dictator who was honest or poor. All dictators are thieves.

When General Videla and his accomplices deposed the constitutional government in 1976, Argentina's external debt was five billion dollars; when the military left, the amount had climbed to almost sixty billion. No one knows precisely where all this money went, but there are some clues. General Albano Harguindeguy was Minister of the Interior during the dictatorship, when his wife found him in an apartment in which he kept a young mistress. Outraged by the infidelity, she started divorce proceedings. In the case that followed she demanded, among other things, half of the forty million dollars that her husband had deposited in a Swiss bank. The Secretary of State for Economic Planning and Coordination, Guillermo Klein, occupied this role from 1976. In 1981 he left this post to represent in Argentina the interests of twenty-two of the foreign banks of Argentina's creditors as a result of Mr. Klein's policies. A year later the military lost the war over the Malvinas/Falklands, which accelerated the downfall of the military rulers. His office was the local representative of the British firm Barclays Bank Limited.

Latin American dictatorships always trumpet their patriotic fervor and nationalism, but they are the necessary accomplices of international banks, which traditionally count on the support and help of the US government, the CIA and the North American embassies. Terence Todman, US Ambassador to the government of Carlos Menem, who continued the policy of the dictatorship, was so influential that they called him "the Viceroy." This sympathetic black guy liked to tell a joke that was in the form of a question: "Why are there no coups d'états in the USA?" The answer: "Because there is no American embassy in the USA." Argentine dictators, like all Latin American dictators, have always been at the service of the thieves from the wealthy countries. In the 1960s US President John Kennedy, passing himself off as a great democrat, implemented the Alliance for Progress, an organization with a declared mission of assisting the development of Latin America, but it was through their missions that dictatorships were established in all countries of the region with the sole exception of Venezuela.

But the practice of using local scoundrels to steal human beings was not invented by Kennedy. In 1939 when an American presidential adviser said the US could not support the Nicaraguan dictator Anastasio Somoza because he was a son of a bitch, Roosevelt replied: "Yes, he's a son of a bitch, but he's our son of a bitch." Inter-national banks were the great thieves, the CIA was the intelligence office, the US embassy was their field marshal, and the local military forces were its armed wing who were given carte blanche to keep the spoils of war. To ensure their operations, they had to terrorize the population, and this required that a formidable enemy be fought utilizing whatever means necessary. Abduction, torture, death and disappearance were the methods chosen by the dictators for that purpose.

But there was a paradox. For the population to be terrorized, they needed to know what could happen to them if they transgressed, meaning that the barbaric acts must be publicized in some way. At the same time the dictators were aware that they were committing crimes that they might someday be held accountable for. With the idea of guaranteeing themselves impunity, they decided to get rid of the bodies of their victims, taking advantage of the legal principle that without a corpus delicti, it is very difficult to get a conviction. The same principle was used by the Nazis in World War II with mixed results, for there is another law: whoever has been in a crime scene always leaves something and takes something. In recent years the torturers, murderers and "desaparecedores" are being prosecuted and jailed. But those who got rich, thanks to these barbaric practices, are still at large and enjoying their ill-gotten gains and have gone unpunished for the destruction of cultures, education and health systems, productive capacity, and the bonds of solidarity among citizens.

Ernesto Mallo

Ernesto Mallo is a self-taught writer, unredeemed and proud of it. To his fortune, God abandoned him as a child so he began writing because it was the only thing he did well at school. He had many different jobs, some not quite legal and others downright subversive but was never caught. He devotes all his honesty to his writing and dedicates a good part of his time to spread the idea that it is necessary to improve the quality and education of criminals given that too often it is they who govern us, while prisons are overcrowded with fools and paupers. His motto: "Better criminals for a better world."

Ernesto works, lives and struggles in Buenos Aires, Argentina. After a longtime as playwright and screenwriter he published five novels: *Needle in the Haystack*, *Sweet Money*, *The Reliquary*, *The History of Water*, and *Men Done You Wrong*. His website is www.ernestomallo.com.ar.

Orwell and the IRA

Ruth Dudley Edwards

I met a friend recently who had spent years covering what in Northern Ireland are euphemistically referred to as the Troubles. "When I was given the job," he said, "I was told that the Provisional IRA were undoubtedly ruthless murderers, but at least you could rely on them to tell the truth. Yet, after a few weeks, I realised that they were the biggest liars I had ever encountered."

When I speak here of the Provisional IRA, who ruled the revolutionary roost from 1972, I include their propaganda wing, Provisional Sinn Féin, for although it is now a successful political party which circumstances have forced into a semblance of democracy, until comparatively recently it was an obedient tool of the Inner Party, the IRA Army Council. And what a Ministry of Truth it constructed! Truly, war became peace, freedom slavery and ignorance strength.

The context was favourable. Nineteenth-century concepts of nationalism drew on a rich seam in the Irish penchant for recording and expressing stories and grievances in poetry, prose and song. And the newest IRA had a ready-made narrative which appeared to justify anti-democratic violence.

Since 1916, when a tiny unelected cabal in Dublin, then a part of the United Kingdom, staged a rebellion and declared soldiers, police and servants of the state—most of them Irish—legitimate targets, successive groups of similar illegality have used violence in the pursuit of an independent, united Ireland ruled by them. At the rebellion's peak there were no more than two thousand in revolt in Dublin and maybe a few hundred involved in skirmishes elsewhere. Casualties were 450: 116 soldiers, 16 police, 76 insurgents, and 242 civilians. Of the 2,600 injured, most were civilians—they almost always are.

The UK was at the time a democracy fighting for survival in Europe. The official response was the execution of sixteen of those they regarded as leaders of the rebellion and the imprisonment, in most cases for a short time, of a few thousand more. These actions were harsh enough to alienate Irish public opinion, notoriously volatile and sentimental, while too mild to smash violent nationalism. Some of those shot were writers who left behind them eloquent essays and poems in defence of their actions that would resonate down the years and give heart to those who wished to emulate them.

Catastrophically, in April 1918 the British government threatened to impose conscription in Ireland, and the backlash brought about the rise of the separatist Sinn Féin and their electoral destruction in December 1918 of constitutional nationalism's Irish Parliamentary Party. Sinn Féin set up an independent national assembly called the Dáil. Although the armistice had removed the conscription threat and Sinn Féin had no mandate for violence, in 1919 another tiny cabal initiated a series of murders of policemen which, being again mainly Irishman against Irishman, precipitated what was a second civil war, known as the War of Independence or Anglo-Irish

War. Around 1,400 died, of whom 624 were from the security forces and 550 the IRA.

The unionist majority in the northern counties of Ireland were prepared to fight to stay out of a nationalist-ruled Ireland, so a treaty with the British government which partitioned Ireland into six counties (Northern Ireland) and twenty-six (the Irish Free State, later the Republic of Ireland) was passed in the Dáil in January 1922. A minority of republicans refused to accept it. The ensuing battle for control of the IRA turned to outright civil war in June after the anti-treatyites had been decisively defeated by the Free State government. In the vicious eleven-month war that followed, seventy-seven republicans were executed by their erstwhile colleagues, 10,000 were jailed or interned, and the 2,000 deaths included a disproportionate number of Protestants, who were the victims of a sectarian campaign.

Ireland settled to an uneasy peace, and most of the irreconcilables accepted the authority of the Dáil. A veil was drawn over the civil war. The poets and the songwriters wrote mainly of the men of 1916 and their fight for Irish freedom and victims of British forces in the War of Independence. Of the 200,000 Irishmen who had fought in the Great War, 30,000 had been killed, but they had become unpersons, erased from existence by the republican thought-police of independent Ireland. Finding themselves in Oceania, the survivors learned quickly to lie low and forget that they had ever fought for Eurasia or Eastasia. Householders knew better than to display photographs of loved ones in British Army uniform.

That recent Irish history had involved the murder, expulsion and intimidation of many thousands who wanted to remain part of the United Kingdom or who simply opposed violent nationalism would rarely be mentioned, for the majority of the population were in the grip of Orwell's blackwhite. Rather than accept that the constitutional nationalism they had overwhelmingly favoured had been driven out of existence by a violence they had never sought, and seeing the revolutionaries in power, they chose to forget what they had believed.

Few would question their children and grandchildren being indoctrinated into accepting that anyone who questioned the validity of the 1916 rising or indeed any pre-1922 violence was deeply unpatriotic. And very few indeed would admit publicly to a British Army relative. Aspiring politicians queued up to claim they had been freedom fighters.

There was no Big Brother poster, but everywhere were images of the executed leaders of 1916, their names adorned the streets of the new Free State, and for many decades they were seen as saints as well as patriots. In terms of political thought, the country was a necrocracy. Although it didn't live up to the unrealistically high principles of the revolutionaries' Proclamation of the Irish Republic, it pretended it did. Photographs of Michael Collins, the assassinated Free State general, joined the iconography.

By now the position of official Ireland—as expressed to this day by those who became known as Fine Gael—was that a) the Irish people had always fought to free themselves of the British yoke, b) the men of 1916 were the founding fathers of the new state, c) Ireland had won a mighty victory over the ancient enemy in 1922, and d) all violence thereafter was unjustified.

When Fianna Fáil, the losing party in the civil war, came to power in 1932, the narrative required adjusting. They were bothered by an IRA rump that despised the

Free State, claimed to be the true inheritors of 1916 and indulged in occasional violence and intimidation. So Fianna Fáil accepted the first three propositions, adapted the fourth to legitimise all political violence until the end of the civil war and banned the IRA. Some of them joined the iconography; their executed brethren were extolled in song.

Since the national narrative of the time was all about resistance to the evil British, the education system dealt with the civil war by never mentioning it. History stopped in January 1922.

In 1939 the surviving hardcore IRA sought help from the Nazis, ran a botched bombing campaign in England, killing a dozen people, and stole weapons from the Irish Army. The government interned and imprisoned more than 1,000, allowed three to die on hunger strike and executed six. A Border Campaign by a revived IRA of 1956–62 resulted in internments and eighteen deaths, which closed the organisation down yet again. Songs continued to be written about new heroes and martyrs.

The Provisional IRA approved of all preceding IRA campaigns and claimed to be finishing the work of 1916 rebels by driving the British out of Northern Ireland and bringing about a united Ireland. Their problem was that the majority of the people of Northern Ireland were British. Over three decades republican paramilitaries killed more than two thousand—five times more than they lost; their loyalist counterparts killed and lost half as many. The security forces killed only 359 and lost more than a thousand, but such was the magnificence of the IRA propaganda machine that those defending the province against terrorists were seen widely as the aggressors.

Beleaguered Ulster Protestants are culturally inclined to call spades spades, to distrust ambiguity, and to lean towards taciturnity or bellicose and defensive rhetoric. Throughout the IRA's attempts to bomb them into a united Ireland, they resisted with great physical and mental courage and assumed that the outside world would realise they were in the right. They are still trying to understand what went wrong.

Meanwhile, to put it in Orwellian terms, the IRA's Ministry of Peace waged a brutal war which it promised would continue forever until true peace was achieved through total victory. It gave the nod to the popular will and gingerly embraced the contesting of elections, but its true intentions were summed up in the memorable 1981 phrase at a Sinn Féin annual conference: "Who here really believes we can win the war through the ballot box? But will anyone here object if, with a ballot paper in one hand and an Armalite in the other, we take power in Ireland?" Minipax waged war by all means available: murder, torture, destruction and now also widespread electoral fraud and coercion.

Oceania had a Youth League and Spies, who loved "the Party and everything connected with it. The songs, the processions, the banners, the hiking, the drilling with dummy rifles, the yelling of slogans, the worship of Big Brother—it was all a sort of glorious game to them." In Oceania Big Brother is the embodiment of the Party. In the IRA the Inner Party or IRA Army Council was fronted by an invisible entity called P. O'Neill, who signed all its statements. As with Mohammed, there were no representations of his face, but the smiling front man of the organisation was Gerry Adams, a member of the Army Council who took blackwhite to new levels of effrontery by claiming never to have been even a foot soldier in the IRA. In the Sinn Féin shops he was on mugs shaking hands with Nelson Mandela; there was even a table lamp fashioned in his image.

As in Oceania, the IRA kept its supporters happy by encouraging them to hate. If they'd had the technology, they'd have organised the daily Two Minutes Hate, but they certainly worked hard on their equivalent of Hate Week. I've attended well-crafted speeches by Sinn Féin luminaries in which the degree of venom directed at unionist politicians, police, soldiers and critics lashed the crowd into a frenzy of loathing. I recall a republican march during the 1990s at a time when maximum propaganda effort was being put into demonising the Royal Ulster Constabulary, whom the IRA were still murdering. Children were dancing alongside, shouting "SS RUC." I stopped a four-year-old and asked him if he knew what "SS" meant. It turned out he didn't even have a clue even about "RUC."

At a time when Sinn Féin were fomenting trouble over Orange parades and working hard at home and abroad to demonise Orangemen, I stood outside City Hall at a Sinn Féin rally and watched a performance by a street-theatre group directed by an IRA terrorist. Now at this time they had taken yet another leaf out of Big Brother's book. ("A new poster had suddenly appeared all over London. It had no caption, and represented simply the monstrous figure of a Eurasian soldier, three or four metres high, striding forward with expressionless Mongolian face and enormous boots, a submachine gun pointed from his hip.") In West Belfast there appeared an enormous mural. Bearing the heading "NOT ALL TRADITIONS DESERVE RESPECT," it featured a hooded and robed Ku Klux Klan horseman with an orange sash riding across a green landscape littered with skulls as well as with rocks daubed with the names of the places where republicans had been trying to provoke Orangemen into a confrontation.

At the front of the stage was a man in an Orange collarette, wearing a Ku Klux Klan hood. In the hearing of hundreds of policemen on duty to defend republicans against angry loyalists, an actor in the uniform of a chief constable and wearing an Orange collarette introduced Constable Baton, Constable Shoot to Kill, and Constable Collusion, all of whom were given a sash and bowler hat. Then came Constable Ever So Nice, with his hand over the mouth of a small, squirming boy over whose head he was trying to thrust an Orange collarette: the lad finally struck him and regained his freedom. The hundreds of children present cheered and cheered.

Minipax's hard work was supplemented by that of the Ministry of Love, which was in charge of rooting out dissidents, malcontents and informers, exiling and maiming those who posed little problem and torturing others until they confessed and pleaded to die. Just as Winston Smith did. Most were murdered; some, later known as the Disappeared, were vaporised.

The Ministry of Plenty demanded that its deprived people be given a larger share of all the good things of life and a higher standard of living. It facilitated smuggling, benefit fraud, counterfeiting, money laundering, robbery, and all manner of ways of impoverishing the state. (The IRA leadership not actually on the run were mainly on state benefits.) Yet Minipax's policy of murdering businessmen and blowing up factories and shops remorselessly destroyed job prospects. As in Oceania, the fruits of its illegal activities were mainly reserved for the Inner and Outer Party; the proles were deliberately kept in poverty. As Emmanuel Goldstein, Oceania's national hate-figure, explained in his banned book, *The Theory and Practice of Oligarchical Collectivism*, prosperity and security would lead the proles "to think for themselves; and when once they had done this, they would sooner or later realise that the privileged minority had no function, and they would sweep it away. In the long run, a hierarchical society was only possible on a basis of poverty and ignorance." The IRA achieved that for a long time; they even discouraged those under their control from reading anything that might challenge their assumptions, lest it encourage them to engage in thoughtcrime.

All the activities of the other ministries created a great deal of work for the IRA's Ministry of Truth, for they had a foreign as well as a domestic audience. Not only did it have the routine job of distorting information, but it also had to represent Minipax's killers as victims and its victims as killers. Thus, a Protestant border farmer who joined a local defence force to protect his family and his village from Catholic terrorists was portrayed as a sectarian militarist and therefore fair game. The strategy of terrorising Catholic policemen succeeded rapidly in making it possible for Minipax to bewail a sectarian police force that tyrannised the minority. Most British governments wanted to be rid of Northern Ireland but felt morally unable to betray the majority, yet their resentful expenditure of blood and treasure was portrayed as self-interested colonialism.

As with Oceania, "the enemy of the moment always represented absolute evil, and it followed that any past or future agreement with him was impossible." This would cause much head-scratching when a beaten IRA—which was pretending it was victorious—had to explain to those outside the Inner Party why they wanted to make peace and why, instead of murdering Protestants, they wished to sit in government with them and make friends. As they began to speak of peace, those who criticised them in any way were dubbed anti-peace and anti-reconciliation. We still are. I was among the journalists who were so branded for suggesting we consider their past actions, their hypocrisy, lies and motives. One of our number, Lindy McDowell, nailed the doublethink with: "Just because I've never killed anyone doesn't mean I'm a bad person."

Just as tricky was the problem that the IRA, like all the preceding IRAs, had claimed they were fighting for Irish unity, yet as a result of their campaign, unionists would not even consider it and even most nationalists north and south no longer wanted it. The Provos could not admit defeat, so they claimed to have been fighting against discrimination and second-class citizenship, yet any objective observer could see that all such grievances had been addressed by 1972.

Blackwhite was the only way to deal with this, but it was unsatisfactory, and only part of the solution to satisfactorily falsifying the past. The Party slogan "Who controls the past controls the future: who controls the present controls the past" is relevant here. The IRA need their defeats to be triumphs, their crimes to be good deeds. Killers as victims was an early propaganda stage.

These days Minitrue has adopted the word "conflict" to describe the Troubles, with the killers being called "combatants," the implication being that everyone caught up in the "conflict" was willingly involved. In Minitrue's world, we are all guilty for the IRA's wicked actions. And the loyalist paramilitaries, the IRA's cynical and willing students, are buying into the same terminology to exculpate themselves. The agents of the state, which battled to defend citizens from terrorism, have become the new terrorists.

A few years ago Gerry Adams offered a classic Minitrue-ism: "I told Mr Blair that the British state has to open up this can of worms and face up to its responsibilities. It has to acknowledge the great hurt it has inflicted on almost a thousand citizens who were killed, and their families who have suffered directly, and all the thousands of others who had their rights undermined and subverted by a policy which encouraged paramilitarism and violence and which in turn corrupted the Protestant working class community." Minitrue were also behind the "Will-he-won't-he?" discussion of whether Martin McGuinness (who ordered the murder of the Queen's cousin and uncle-in-law, Lord Mountbatten), would be prepared to overcome his great hurt over Bloody Sunday in 1972 (which he may or may not have instigated) and shake hands with her.

Minitrue do a fine job. Their lawyers are permanently on the qui vive to spot opportunities for libel proceedings, and the media, with limited money, frequently cave in. When Thomas "Slab" Murphy, the IRA's Chief of Staff, sued the *Sunday Times* for claiming he was a smuggler and an IRA member, the paper stood up to him. He lost, there was an appeal, and the enormous costs were awarded against him. More than a decade later, he hasn't paid a penny. Few newspapers have pockets as deep as that.

These days Minitrue have a technical unit that, for instance, alters disobliging entries on Wikipedia, so, as much as possible, they are controlling the present and the past. But there's an even bigger challenge. Once Sinn Féin went into a power-sharing government in Northern

Ireland and attempted to appear as respectable as befits a would-be coalition partner in the Republic, they had to disown anyone who behaved as they had done. So, like the IRAs before them, they announced that violence had been legitimate up until the time they gave it up. But yet again, there are hardcore revolutionaries who don't agree, and even when denounced by erstwhile heroes, they have had the temerity to shoot, bomb, mutilate, and do other criminal acts in the name of Ireland.

As Fine Gael, Fianna Fáil, the Provos and all the others did in their time, they trace their legitimacy back to the anti-democratic cabal that began the carnage in Dublin in 1916. They call in aid Patrick Pearse, the President of the Provisional Republic, whose portrait was behind the desk of Taoiseach Bertie Ahern even as he was pleading with the Real IRA, the murderers of Omagh, to give up. "We have no misgivings, no self-questionings," wrote Pearse. "While others have been doubting, timorous, ill-at-ease, we have been serenely at peace with our consciences ... We called upon the names of the great confessors of our national faith, and all was well with us. Whatever soul-searchings there may be among Irish political parties now or hereafter, we go on in the calm certitude of having done the clear, clean, sheer thing. We have the strength and peace of mind of those who never compromise."

All those who believe that the men of 1916 were justified but that one can pick and choose which of their heirs have a right to kill are engaged in doublethink: they're accepting two mutually contradictory beliefs as correct. Generations of Irish politicians have laboured to avoid this truth. In doing so, they created the conditions in which Orwellian liars of the stature of the Provisional IRA/Sinn Féin could flourish.

Ruth Dudley Edwards

Ruth Dudley Edwards's non-fiction includes biographies of Patrick Pearse, Victor Gollancz and newspapermen Hugh Cudlipp and Cecil King, as well as the history of *The Economist*, a portrait of Ulster Orangemen, and *Aftermath: The Omagh Bombing and the Families' Pursuit of Justice* (long-listed for the Orwell Prize). Her latest satirical crime novel, *Killing the Emperors*, targets conceptual art.

Doublethink for the Arab Spring

Matt Rees

In the Brazil neighborhood of Rafah's refugee camp, yards from the border between the Gaza Strip and Egypt, I entered the National Institute for Development and Services. Usually Palestinian businesses took names that told you exactly what they did. My favorite was the less-than-snappy Gaza Company for the Importation of Egyptian Consumer Goods. In the case of this National Institute, the name was, to say the least, misleading. This business place was the den of one of the town's leading smugglers.

Fayez showed me into his office. I sat on one of the black leather sofas, of which there were at least two more than necessary in a room of this size, cramped around Fayez's big horseshoe-shaped ebony desk. Red plush carpet covered the walls. There were boxes of electronic equipment piled in the corners and in the corridor. The room reminded me of the lounges of seedy recording studios I had known in New York City, male and unkempt and decorated with more money than sense or taste. A deaf-mute teenager held up a teacup. Fayez, who was in his mid-thirties, nodded and wiggled his hand, signaling the youth to prepare the tea with a medium amount of sugar.

For more than a decade the government of Gaza has either ceased to function or been in the hands of Hamas, which is at best kept at arm's length by most countries. So Fayez's business is, indeed, a bringer of development and services. "Goods that people can get here legally in Rafah are at a lower level than anywhere in the world, except maybe Afghanistan," he said.

Gunmen and smugglers have brought disaster down upon the heads of their fellow Gazans because they have needed the cover of war against Israel or against each other for their criminal operations. They were demonstrably awful men, violent, coercive, and ruthless. But you wouldn't know that from reading most of what's written about them by international journalists. The contemporary foreign correspondent is a castrato of even-handedness. You can't write about a criminal operating in Rafah without mentioning that he might be a legitimate businessman if Israel would only make the people of Gaza free. In the polarities of the Middle East "debate," Big Brother looms at the end of a fiber-optic cable. No matter what ignoramus zaps his spite into the office of a magazine editor, he's treated as if he were an authority. The childish fear engendered in the editor is passed along to the correspondent in subtle signals to shake no trees, to attempt to please everyone and, thus, to anger everyone.

I left Fayez and went northwards from Rafah along the Saladin Road that travels the length of the Gaza Strip. I knew the route well: the sycamore-lined avenue through Khan Yunis near the UN Relief and Works Agency school, where it always seemed to be time for the kids to flood home, teetering forward beneath their enormous, colorful backpacks and laughing at me, the tall foreigner, when I stopped to buy a Coke; Deir el-Balah, where the road was shaded by wondrously soaring date palms; the rolling final stage into Gaza City over the dunes. Each of the towns I passed through along the length of the Gaza Strip had its own character, but somehow the same predicaments pertained. Sometimes people would say that certain towns had a particular political bent: that Khan Yunis, for example, tended to support the Popular Front for the Liberation of Palestine (PFLP) more than other places. Violence broke down those assumptions. If Khan Yunis aligned with the PFLP before 2000, then the onset of the intifada saw the PFLP hardmen ally themselves with Fatah and Democratic Front gunmen; others who had never before been involved in politics joined Hamas; and yet others who had always been nothing more than criminals gained legitimacy through espousing political hatred. Violence and threat made men powerful. Ideology broke down beneath the onslaught of the Israeli army and the toll it took on the thinkers and experienced activists among the Palestinians as they were arrested or assassinated, leaving their foot soldiers filled with fear and anger, burning for any kind of revenge for its own sake rather than as part of a political or religious program, and heavily armed. Those who were left may genuinely have taken to their political groupings out of a desire to carry on the struggle against Israel, but plenty of the new men saw their chance to use the established local factions as personal power bases.

Adnan Shahine, for one, had no such power base. Which is why he's dead.

The Shahines were eating the *iftar* meal to break their fast at the end of another day of Ramadan during the years of the intifada. Almost nightly, local gunmen went to the edge of the city, to a village of mostly middle-class

Palestinian Christians called Beit Jala, and fired across the deep wadi at the Israeli apartment blocks in the Jerusalem suburb of Gilo. In turn the Israelis would dispatch their helicopters overhead and, as their rotors churned, the reverberations would rumble through the cloudy winter nights like thunder to the very opposite end of Bethlehem, to the Saff neighborhood in the southwest of town where the Shahines shared their evening meal.

Jalila Shahine handed her thirty-eight-year-old son a flat, yellow pancake to mop up the gravy on his plate. She was proud of Adnan, a housepainter who had spent years in Israeli jails for his membership in Fatah. Slight and black-bearded, he sat beside his two wives. The first had given him two boys and two girls; he had married a second, Haifa, who was twenty-four, a month ago and already she was pregnant. It was news of this grandchild that made Jalila Shahine feel the greatness of this breakfast even more than usual.

There was a knock at the door. "Adnan, go and see who it is," Jalila said. The meal continued. There was no sound, no voice loud enough for Jalila to hear, though the front door was only a couple of yards across the hall from the dining room. When Adnan didn't return, Jalila went to look. She noticed that the door was open but Adnan was not there. Then she saw him on the steps outside. There were two men with him, and she felt a strange stab of shock; they wore black balaclava helmets, stocking masks with eyes and mouth cut out, and they were armed. The town was full of rumors of Israeli undercover units. Maybe Adnan was involved in operations against the Israelis, and one of the undercover squads had come for him. "What's going on?" Jalila said.

"He's wanted by General Intelligence," one of the men said. He wore the turquoise and black camouflage pants of the Palestinian police's Rapid Reaction Force and carried a pistol. His accent was authentic; he was no Israeli. The other man, who wore a pair of jeans, carried a Kalashnikov.

"Why? Why's he wanted?" Jalila said.

"Look, the jeep is down the hill, waiting," the man said to Jalila, gesturing impatiently along the empty street. He nudged Adnan. "Let's go."

Adnan slipped on his shoes, which he had left on the top step outside the front door. The man with the pistol gripped Adnan's left arm. They got to the bottom of the steps. Jalila looked around; she didn't see the jeep they mentioned. Now the gunmen each grasped one of Adnan's arms, marching him down the hill, his hands bound in plastic cuffs that she hadn't noticed at first. Jalila followed with Adnan's new wife, Haifa. "Why did you handcuff him?" They walked faster. Jalila thought of asking a neighbor for help, but the street was deserted; everyone was breaking their fast or praying at the mosque.

Jalila caught up again. She saw panic on Adnan's face now. She sensed that he knew the identity of these two men in the masks and that the situation had become more serious than he had first thought.

"Don't leave me, Mother!" he said.

"Shut up!" said the man with the pistol. He turned on Jalila, who was tall for a Palestinian woman and strongly built. "And you, go home," he said to the mother and the wife.

"I'm not going to leave him. You can shoot me, but I won't leave," Jalila said.

The man with the pistol halted for a second, as though coming to a decision, and then he moved. He pulled Adnan to the middle of the narrow street and pushed him to his knees. Adnan began to sob. "I'm warning you, go back to your house," the man shouted at Jalila.

"I'm not going," she said.

The two gunmen walked seven yards away from Jalila's quivering son. Quickly, the first raised his pistol and fired. The bullet hit Adnan in the left shoulder. When it struck, he was looking at his wife and mother and, despite the impact, his pleading eyes stayed on them. The gunmen stepped a few yards farther away and the pistol fired again. This time, it blasted into Adnan Shahine's neck and he fell dead. By the time Jalila reached Adnan, the gunmen were away down an alley.

Jalila Shahine fell to her knees. She reached her hands to heaven and called out to God. She dipped her hands in the blood that ran from Adnan's neck and smeared it across her cheeks and forehead. "God is most great, *Allahu akbar.*"

"Come out, all of you!" she cried to her neighbors. None paid attention. No door opened.

The gunmen who killed Adnan Shahine soon published their version of why he died, spreading it through the networks of activists in Bethlehem. Adnan was slain, according to them, because he worked as a collaborator with Israel. They said he had guided an Israeli assassination squad on an operation a few days before his death.

The story that Shahine was a collaborator, which in itself was hard enough for a foreigner like me to uncover, was not the real explanation. For months it seemed to me the most likely reason, until I finally met a man who knew the secrets of Fatah in Bethlehem and whose integrity I did not doubt. I asked him about Shahine. He remembered the case.

"Was he a collaborator with Israel?" I said.

"No," the Fatah man said.

"So why did they kill him?"

The man smiled bitterly and breathed a long stream of cigarette smoke.

"Because they wanted to show they could kill a collaborator."

The gunmen saw that Israel's hit squads were starting to strike at them. Some of that success was based on information gathered from the Shin Bet's network of Palestinian collaborators. The gunmen had to kill one of those collaborators so that other informers would think twice before helping the Israelis. But the gunmen didn't know the identity of any collaborators. That meant they had to kill someone who wasn't really a collaborator and put it about that he had been an informant. The gunmen couldn't pick a victim from a prominent, powerful family because the relatives would demand tribal retribution. So they chose Adnan Shahine, whose clan was small and weak. And they killed him.

That was it. I found it so astonishing that I asked my Fatah contact to reprise the reasoning three times. Then I stopped because I feared that if I heard it once more, it might start to make sense.

In the doublethink that had descended upon the Palestinians as their society turned in on itself, there was no need for a Room 101, no need for the confession that breaks a man before his lonely death. Stalin needed show trials. The gunmen of Bethlehem needed a dead body in the street.

In Bethlehem the Ta'amra tribe ran the rackets and staffed the ranks of the gunmen. They lived in outlying villages. Most were from the Abayat family. Only sixty years of settled village life separated the Abayat Ta'amra from their nomadic desert history, and they still followed tribal law. One night soon after Adnan Shahine died, a crowd of Abayats showed up outside Bethlehem's jail, where five accused collaborators were held. One of the collaborators, Muhammed Nawawra, confessed to helping the Israelis assassinate Hussein Abayat, a leading gunman. Though there was no doubt that the courts would deliver a merciless sentence upon Nawawra, the Abayats repeatedly tried to break into the jail to lynch him.

One of the local leaders of the gunmen in Bethlehem was Ahmed al-Mughrabi, who sent Muhammed Daraghmeh to blow himself up at the age of eighteen. Daraghmeh died in Jerusalem's religious Jewish neighborhood of Beit Yisrael in April 2002, killing nine Israelis, including an entire family. Muhammed was a carpenter. He installed cherrywood kitchen cabinets for my wife's cousin. There was little work because of the intifada, so he took a job in a butcher's shop. No one in his family understood that it was not only in his daily work that he was reduced to slaughter.

On the day Muhammed Daraghmeh died, his mother Ibtisam was watching the television news on the second floor of the family's roughly built home on a narrow hilltop street in the Dehaisha refugee camp near Bethlehem. It was 9:30 p.m. She had not seen Muhammed since that morning, when he had been playing with his sisters as Ibtisam washed dishes. The news flashed a report about a bombing in Jerusalem. Then a group of Fatah gunmen started shooting into the air outside the family's house. Ibtisam's husband, Ahmed, went outside to find out why they were firing. He came back, his face white. Ibtisam fainted and was taken to the hospital. She was injected with a sedative and received an insulin shot for her diabetes. Four hours later, when she came home, she was speechless, weeping uncontrollably and silently.

Muhammed's brother Amr approached her and tried to kiss her cheeks. "Is Muhammed martyred?" she managed to ask him. Amr nodded. Ibtisam fainted again.

Two weeks later a neighbor named Um Sabri came round in the evening to pay a condolence call on Ibtisam. Um Sabri said, "I wish I was Muhammed's mother, so that I could say that my son is a martyr." Ibtisam began to cry. She couldn't stop. Amr was angry at Um Sabri, angry at this bullshit rhetoric. He wanted to tell the woman that his mother had been in shock ever since Muhammed's death and that there was no pleasure in having a martyr in the family. He kicked Um Sabri out of the house. But he couldn't get her to take the word "martyr" with her. It's intended to be a word of consolation and heroism and inspiration. For me it has always represented the highly sexual perversity of Christian martyrdom: wan Saint Sebastian filled full of holes by the arrows of his burly tormentors like a buggered boy, or Saint Agatha with her tits cut off as if she'd been butchered in a snuff film. "Martyr" is a word that has been whitewashed in the West by centuries of Catholic sexual repression and nationalistic cant of the kind Orwell so castigated. In the modern Muslim world, it's a means willfully to ignore the evident betrayal of ordinary fighters by the corrupt powerful.

Before Muhammed Daraghmeh went to Jerusalem, he shaved his head to look like a hip young Israeli. Then he put on a black and white keffiyeh, tied like a bandanna around his forehead, and posed with a Kalashnikov while Ahmed al-Mughrabi recorded his "martyrdom message" on videotape. As he read his final statement, Muhammed lifted the assault rifle, resting the butt on his hip. He looked down at the text of his message as he read it. His face was soft and a light bronze color.

Ibtisam didn't recognize him when she saw the footage. The bomb maker, al-Mughrabi, sold the broadcast rights for Muhammed's martyrdom message to an Arab satellite news station for $10,000. He split the cash with an officer in Palestinian General Intelligence who helped prepare Muhammed's mission.

There was no consciousness among the gunmen of the suffering they might cause. In May 2003 Palestinian police arrested a ring of bank robbers who also happened to be members of the Popular Front for the Liberation of Palestine. The police held the robbers at their Bethlehem lockup. The night after the arrests, PFLP gunmen went to Beit Jala and fired shots across the wadi toward Gilo. It had been a year since anyone had opened fire on the Jerusalem suburb because it had become clear there was no military or political gain to doing so. But the PFLP had found a rationale. They wanted to draw the Israelis into an invasion of the whole of Bethlehem, knowing that the Palestinian police always emptied their jails on those occasions so that the Israelis wouldn't be able to take all the prisoners away for interrogation. To secure the freedom of their partners in crime, the gunmen were ready to see an entire town cowering behind closed doors as enemy tanks patrolled the streets. It was another illustration of terrorist action apparently aimed at Israel that in fact was driven by an internal Palestinian dispute.

The Aqsa Martyrs' Brigades gunmen sent boys like Muhammed Daraghmeh to die among Israelis while they strutted around Bethlehem. They possessed guns and money. The only element of gangster chic they lacked was women. They found that in a tiny stone house above an olive grove on the steep hill of Sidr, a neighborhood at the edge of Beit Jala. Even by the repulsive standards of the Martyrs' Brigades, what they did there was appalling.

Rada Amaro lived in that house. She was twenty-four, beautiful, tall, with stylishly bobbed black hair. Her eyes made the exotic, long-lashed ovals that Westerners find so alluring and mysterious in Oriental women when they are framed, coyly, by a veil. But Rada wore no veil. As a Christian she was free to dress more daringly, and she took that license to the limit, even a little beyond. At Peter's, a hair salon where she worked in Beit Jala, she would wear tops that by conservative Palestinian standards exposed a good deal of her smooth, ochre shoulders and even a little cleavage. There were other things that she exposed at the salon: a client once gave her money for her family, when Rada told her times were hard for the Amaros. Rada and her eighteen-year-old sister Dunya lived with their aging parents. Moussa Amaro, their father, was seventy-two and had been without a job for years. His other four daughters were married, as was one of his sons. His second boy, Jeriez, made a scant wage as a glazier and lived with his parents in the old blockhouse, the poorest dwelling in an otherwise middle-class area. Moussa's wife brought home a small wage from her cleaning job at the Talitha Kumi School, which was run by German Protestants.

It was a dull existence for a beautiful young girl who knew about the excitement the world could offer from television but who had no opportunity to escape her dead-end life through further education. The way she dressed and her girlish flirtatiousness was sufficient to bring Rada Amaro a reputation as a woman of loose morals in the puritan world of the Palestinians. Even though she was from the Christian minority and not bound by the strictures of Muslim society, neighbors judged her negatively simply because she stood out. Stood out enough to attract the attention of the Abayats.

Two of the gunmen's leaders began to have sex with Rada Amaro, according to people close to the Martyrs' Brigades in Bethlehem. However it began, the girl undoubtedly was scared to say no to men feared by the whole town. She could turn to no one. She was a Christian and therefore lacked the tight social backing that might have protected a Muslim woman in the refugee camps. Her family was poor, so she didn't have even the moderate clout that a wealthy Christian clan might have been able to muster. Some other Martyrs' Brigades gunmen tried to rape a Christian woman in Beit Sahour, a suburb on the other side of Bethlehem from Beit Jala; the woman's father was wealthy enough to send her to safety in Jordan. Moussa Amaro was powerless and penniless. Once it started, there was no way out for Rada. If Rada had tried to stop sleeping with the Abayats, she would have feared they might hurt her. Even if they let her go, they could ruin her chances of ever finding a husband by letting it be known what she had done. Her reputation had already been bad enough when she'd done nothing more than wear sexy clothing.

In the end the decision was not Rada Amaro's to make. Just as the Martyrs' Brigades gunmen used Adnan Shahine to show that they would be merciless on collaborators, they decided Rada could serve to boost their moral standing among the public. Two gunmen went to the Sidr blockhouse. It was the time of the afternoon when the heat was slow on the dusty hill and the grasshoppers susurrated in the olive grove below the Amaros' home. The gunmen found Rada there alone. They put her on the bed and covered her face with a pillow. They shot her through the pillow. Before they left, her sister Dunya came home unexpectedly. They forced her onto the bed next to her sister and shot her through another pillow. At four p.m. Moussa Amaro found his two daughters with bullets in their heads.

The Martyrs' Brigades issued a statement. They asserted their responsibility for the killing of the two Amaro girls. "We wanted to clean the Palestinian house of prostitutes," the statement said. The Martyrs' Brigades thugs sexually degraded Rada Amaro, punished her for it and then claimed the position of moral champions from a society that they more than anyone were responsible for sullying. There's little difference between the tawdriness of small-time hoods like the Abayats and the dictator at the head of his disgusting little state. The dictator can salt away billions and get away with it longer, perhaps. Both want the same things. Saddam Hussein raped women, and so did the Abayats. Muammar Ghaddafi ended up dead at a roadside. So did the Abayats.

Within a few months the two Abayats who murdered Rada Amaro were dead, slain by an Israeli helicopter missile while driving a stolen jeep. Palestinian officials expressed outrage at Israel's killing of the two men, though the same political leaders never had anything to say about the death of Rada Amaro at the hands of gangsters on their payroll. Foreign correspondents scrutinized the morality of Israel's assassination policy, as so often before. But when I talked to the people of Bethlehem, I found they saw a pitiless justice in the end of the Abayats. Unlike Rada Amaro, those who tormented her merited their violent demise. Despite the efforts of local gangsters or national dictators, there will always be some places in a man's heart that keep within their silence an awareness of what their world could be.

Matt Rees

Matt Rees is an award-winning crime novelist who lives in Jerusalem. The French magazine L'Express called him "the Dashiell Hammett of Palestine." As a journalist, Rees covered the Middle East for over a decade. Yasser Arafat once tried to have him arrested, but Matt eluded him to write his novels. He was born in Newport, Wales, and studied at Oxford University and the University of Maryland. He published a nonfiction account of Israeli and Palestinian society called *Cain's Field: Faith, Fratricide, and Fear in the Middle East* in 2004 (Free Press). He won the prestigious Crime Writers Association John Creasey New Blood Dagger in 2008. He has written six crime novels which have been sold to leading publishers in 24 countries. His latest novels are fictionalized unravelings of real historical mysteries, *Mozart's Last Aria* and *A Name in Blood*, which is about the death of Caravaggio. His website is mattrees.net.

Killing Fields Justice: A Witness to History

Christopher G. Moore

ECCC Court Complex

At 9:00 a.m. on Monday, 21 November 2011, the beige curtains were slowly peeled back before an audience of roughly six hundred people. The moment was like something out of *The Wizard of Oz*: high expectations of what is behind the curtain, manipulating the levers of power, inevitably result in disappointment. Three men in their eighties sat on the right side of the chambers. Each of the trio was charged with crimes against humanity, genocide and violations of the Geneva Convention.

Along with Pol Pot, these men had been top Khmer Rouge policymakers. As the political architects of the campaign of death and destruction that defined the Khmer Rouge, they were on trial before a court of law. Seated with the accused, their black-gowned lawyers listened to the charges against their clients. Uniformed security personnel kept the accused under a watchful eye.

At 9:05 a.m. everyone on both sides of the glass enclosure stood as seven robed judges filed in and took their places on the bench. Four of the judges were

Cambodian; the remaining three were from New Zealand, Austria and France. As the court was called to order, everyone in the court and gallery took their seats. Case 2 had commenced. History was being made.

As a law professor and a lawyer, I have experienced the ritual of courtrooms in Canada, the United States, England, Malaysia and Thailand, with the opposing counsel at their tables, the judges on the bench, and the accused in the dock. Courtrooms are a form of ancient theatre, where the players have defined roles, the procedures are formal, and the decor is somber. Objective, fair, rational decision making is the premise for the deliberation. Justice is the goal. Everyone is assigned a role to play.

The Extraordinary Chambers in the Courts of Cambodia (ECCC) was specifically built for the trial of the men and women who occupied leadership positions during the Khmer Rouge reign of terror. The courtroom physically separated its participants and the audience with a large wall of glass. Inside the fishbowl were the officials, judges, lawyers, and security personnel.

Courts are public storytelling venues, where the prosecution carries the burden of telling the story to establish guilt. On this Monday the prosecution laid out its case. On the Tuesday the accused made opening arguments in their defense. They denied their responsibility for the crimes of which they were accused. As the trial proceeded, they would call witnesses and entered evidence to establish a counter-narrative, such as that they acted to repel foreign invaders and to safeguard Cambodia. Over the months and years to follow, the prosecution would introduce evidence supporting the charges. Then, the accused, given an opportunity to present their side of the story, would continue to refuse to accept that they had done anything wrong. This denial would come as no surprise, as it matched the mindset that had formulated the policies that led to the Killing Fields.

I hadn't come here to witness a "normal" murder trial. Not even the trial of the worst serial killer could approach the body count attributed to the policies of these three men. Their crimes were an order of magnitude beyond anyone's experience of homicide cases. The systematic killing had seen the scaling of murder to an industrial level. Men, women and children by the truckload were murdered day after day, for years, with no break between the killings.

I observed the accused over the course of the proceedings as the Cambodian co-prosecutor read her opening statement. The audience was filled with ordinary Cambodians. They had come to see the Khmer Rouge leaders whose policies had visited death upon nearly every Cambodian family. Ordinary Cambodians, students, relatives of victims and survivors all sat side by side in the audience to gaze upon the faces of the men who had unleashed the nightmare. The proceedings were also broadcast throughout Cambodia. People in the remote countryside and in the cities and towns could watch on television or listen on the radio. The entire population of Cambodia finally had their chance after thirty-two years to hear details of the charges laid against the three accused. This was far more than a legal proceeding; it was a place where those who had brought about the Killing Fields would be judged.

Not many had ever thought that day would come. Or, if it did, that they would witness the proceedings. Yet there they were, watching, remembering, coming to terms with the past and searching the faces of those on the other side of the glass for answers.

The Historical Context

Speaking truth to power has always been a rare event at any time, anywhere in the world. Those in power like to control information, shape the narrative, and eliminate rival versions of the event. They use their power to control, monitor and supervise the movement of millions of people. Most of the time, such power operates virtually undetected in the background. We hardly notice the way government policies require us to move one way as opposed to another. When power went off the rails in Cambodia, and mass murder became the policy, the role of Khmer Rouge leaders became a powerful parable of the sort of radical ideological purity that can quickly lead to hell on earth.

Those who have sought to challenge authority have historically paid a heavy price. The case of Cambodia illustrates what happens when power and authority become detached and unbounded by normal values, ethics, beliefs or customs, and degenerates into a vast killing machine.

When I first traveled to Cambodia in March 1993, it was as a correspondent to cover the United Nations Transitional Authority in Cambodia (UNTAC) operation. From March 1992 to September 1993, about 22,000 troops from around the world were sent to police a process of ceasefire monitoring, election oversight and political rehabilitation. Civil war continued, with the Khmer Rouge holed up in the northwestern part of the country, near the Thai border. It had been fourteen years since the Khmer Rouge had been chased out of Phnom Penh. While UNTAC forces created the platform of stability that would be essential for rebuilding a new government structure and holding elections, the continuing armed struggle, which lasted for years after

UNTAC left, worked to the advantage of the Khmer Rouge by delaying their day of reckoning.

What no one envisioned in 1993 was that those responsible for the Khmer Rouge regime would be held accountable for their crimes against humanity and genocide. More than eighteen years after I first reported on the UNTAC operation in Cambodia, I returned to witness the opening day of Case 2 in a hybrid court. The structure, operation and selection of the court personnel were experimental. The hybrid court was the result of a joint venture, bringing together international judges and principles of law with those of Cambodia. The intention was to create a venue that would have legitimacy based on universal principles and would recognize Cambodian local laws, values and interest. Legitimacy is the key requirement in undertakings of this kind. The court has to be accepted, not just by the international community, but also by the Cambodians.

The ECCC is UN-supported and funded but was established by Cambodian legislation. Can such a hybrid judicial system fulfill its promise to deliver justice that will satisfy the international community without destabilizing the political realities in contemporary Cambodia? The trial is a test of whether such a court structure is workable.

The alternative would have been sending the accused off to The Hague for trial. While that might have better guaranteed the enforcement of international legal principles, it would have deprived the victims and their families of an opportunity to witness the trial firsthand and to see for themselves the faces of the accused. Also, the existing court structure has come up with a unique blending of public and private interests. The proceedings are inclusive in a way that hasn't been attempted before in war crime trials. In Cambodia thousands of individual civil complainants have lodged their cases with the courts. The civilian cases will proceed along with the public cases before the same panel of judges.

For Cambodians Case 2 signals a significant political message: high-level government officials can be made to stand trial for certain types of policies. On opening day that message was graphic. The Khmer Rouge policymakers were in the dock. They had been arrested and detained. They were being compelled to explain their actions and rebut evidence of their crimes. In many parts of the world, Southeast Asia included, the highest levels of political leadership have historically remained above the law and untouchable. For crimes against humanity and genocide, their traditional shield of immunity had now been stripped away. That is in itself a breathtaking idea for many in Cambodia and the region.

Previously, there had been no mechanism to make the political strongmen yield to principles of fairness, justice and equality. Policies by such leaders were left unchallenged, or those who sought to challenge them were imprisoned, exiled or murdered. On Monday, 21 November, history turned a page on such immunity. Those who were once too powerful ever to be questioned were now standing trial and facing life sentences if convicted.

The Statistics of Murder

The history of the Khmer Rouge is often reduced to a discussion of cold numbers. Pol Pot, Brother No. 1, escaped trial by dying in a Khmer Rouge enclave inviting speculation as to the circumstances of his death. Nuon Chea, Brother No. 2, is on trial in Case 2. The designations of the cases brought before the ECCC are talked about in shorthand numerical code: Case 1 resulted in the conviction of Kaing Guek Eav, alias Duch. Case 2 is still ongoing. As for Cases 3 and 4, which would place in the dock the operational commanders who carried out the genocide (and it is unlikely either Case 3 or 4 will go to trial due to political reasons). Journalists, court officials and judges all resort to the number game when discussing the history of the cases.

"It is doubtful 3 and 4 will proceed," was a frequently voiced opinion among the court officials and journalists I spoke with.

"Number 2 is the essential case as it focuses on those responsible for the Khmer Rouge's policies."

The number of people who died during the Khmer Rouge period—of starvation, disease, exhaustion and execution—is estimated to be between 1.7 and 2.2 million. Eight hundred thousand are thought to have been executed. Our top mathematicians, like Professor John Paulos of Temple University, warn newspaper readers to be on guard when journalists use big, round numbers. We must be cautious with such numbers, knowing the potential for inaccuracy is great. Let's be honest. We can't ever know with certainty the real number of people buried in the thousands of Killing Fields inside Cambodia.

One court official told me that forced marriages (one of the charges under the category of Crimes against Humanity) numbered in the tens of thousands. Another said there were 350,000 such marriages. There are reports of 250,000 women who were forced into marriage by the Khmer Rouge. The sad reality is no one can verify the numbers or, in the case of forced marriages, even the range of numbers at issue.

The overall death toll of Cambodians during this period is another example of a large number range. So many

Khmers and members of ethnic minorities died during the Pol Pot period that the best estimate of fatalities has nearly a thirty percent margin of error. Another number is that twenty-five percent of the Cambodian population during this period lost their lives. Again, no one knows or will ever know the real figure. Numbers are also an abstraction. They represent people and lives but they don't have faces, families, dreams, hopes, friends. The shadows of the real people have receded into the distance behind the numbers.

To fully appreciate the impact of these events on the Cambodian population, it is useful to place the twenty-five percent death rate into a larger, global perspective. Killing a quarter of a country's population translates to over 75 million Americans dead, 300 million Chinese, 300 million Indians, 20 million Germans, 17.5 million Thais or 47.5 million Brazilians. The numbers are staggering.

In addition, the Khmer Rouge targeted the educated urban population, including lawyers, judges, doctors, business people, artists, writers, students, teachers, civil servants, intellectuals, and monks. There is a story of a Cambodian along the road when an official car pulled up along side. He used the French greeting *bonjour* to the occupants inside and was greeted back in French. Later, a Khmer Rouge cadre arrived to arrest the man and he was subsequently executed. As in George Orwell's *Animal Farm*, some animals were more equal than others. Some were entitled to speak French, and for others French was a death sentence. One effect of the killing of this class of people was to cripple the ability to create an institutional mechanism to oppose state-sponsored murder. The Khmer Rouge ruthlessly killed all opposition.

The delay in justice is in part explained by the fact that the class of qualified people needed to administer justice was systematically eliminated. It wasn't only that the justice system collapsed, but also that the network of people who staffed the previous political, social and economic system had been exterminated. To this day there are very few university-trained judges in Cambodia. The damage done by the Khmer Rouge has not been fully repaired after more than a generation.

Search for the Truth and Justice

One purpose of this type of international trial for war crimes is to provide psychological aid and comfort to the traumatized survivors. It isn't simply a means to establish the guilt of the parties charged but a way for the victims to come to terms with their past. The big questions are asked during such a trial. Who among the leaders was responsible for the policies and who should be held accountable? What is the truth behind conflicting evidence, and what manner of justice is sufficient, given the enormity of the crimes?

On the morning of 21 November, Cambodian co-prosecutor Chea Leang, a woman with a master's degree in law from a German university, opened with the case against three senior Khmer Rouge leaders: Nuon Chea, Ieng Sary and Khieu Samphan. Her task was to outline the case to be tried over the next couple of years against the three accused.

A fourth accused, Ieng Thirith, wasn't in the courtroom on Monday. A couple of days earlier, her case had been severed from the other three. The ECCC acted on evidence that Ieng Thirith now suffered from Alzheimer's disease, which interfered with her ability to participate in the proceedings. Ieng Thirith studied English in Paris and was a Shakespearean scholar. In the preliminary proceedings before the start of the trial, Ieng

Thirith had a history of ranting and raving in a King Lear-like way. Her voice won't be heard during the current round of trials, given her mentally unstable condition. Whether she will ever be tried is in doubt.

With the exit of Ieng Thirith, that left three elderly men (all in their eighties) sitting motionless in the courtroom, listening to the litany of charges against them. It was a chance to look directly at the faces of the men responsible for such death and suffering. They sat impassively throughout the opening statement, as they listened to the charges brought against them. There were no outbursts, no signs of emotional reaction. Nuon Chea's eyes were hidden behind dark sunglasses. As with professional poker players, their faces weren't betraying their feelings, whatever they were.

At an ECCC press conference on the Sunday before the trial, court officials estimated the length of the trial to be approximately two years—that is, if everything were to go according to plan. Add another year for the appeals process, and the final verdict shouldn't be expected before November 2014. Given the age of the accused trio, it will be a race against time to see that justice is done before actuarial realities come into play.

Pol Pot, Brother No. 1, died in 1998, a true believer and defiant to the end. As the proceedings opened, it was not known whether his colleagues on trial would take a similar stance on their involvement in policy formulation and implementation, or whether they would, like Duch, the head of the infamous S-21 Security Center, admit their guilt. By day two it was clear that the three men, like Pol Pot, would not admit guilt and would defend their actions.

Destruction of the Family Unit

Women have been relegated to the status of second-class citizens in a number of the ten Southeast Asian countries, and Cambodia is no exception. The status of a second-class citizen is a different category, however, from that of women who lived under the Khmer Rouge regime.

What made Chea Leang's opening statement by turns moving, horrifying and numbing was her overview of the actions of the Khmer Rouge in carrying out the policies of the Pol Pot regime. The fact that a Khmer woman lawyer was chosen to give the opening statement was rich with symbolism. It shouldn't be lost on those being tried that the Khmer Rouge regime had systematically violated women, destroyed their traditions of marriage and family structure, forced them to marry and worked them to death in fields and on infrastructure projects. Given the humiliation and arbitrary treatment, and the gross violation of human rights, it was ironic that the Khmer men in the dock should hear the list of their crimes read out by a legally trained Khmer woman. During their reign of terror, she certainly would have been killed.

The image that comes to mind is that of the youths portrayed in Golding's *Lord of the Flies*. The rank-and-file Khmer Rouge were no more than children. The average age of the Khmer Rouge troops that entered Phnom Penh in 1975 was seventeen years old. Like the children in *Lord of the Flies*, they carried out their tasks with a rapacious brutality. Children no longer under parental restraint easily fall into systematic and arbitrary violence. The three co-defendants were part of an "adult" leadership that, in formulating policies, orchestrated the movement of the rank and file who did the actual killing.

Where were the parents of these Khmer Rouge child soldiers? They were absent.

An unusual but important aspect of the charge of crimes against humanity concerns the Khmer Rouge policy of forced marriages. The numbers are again in conflict, but it is not disputed that forced marriage was a widespread practice during the period between 17 April 1975 and 6 January 1979. The figure of 250,000 Khmer women who were forced to marry a partner under the policies of the Khmer Rouge regime, though unverifiable, is an indication of the scope of the policy. Forced marriages were part of a policy of systematically destroying the traditional courtship ritual and directly assaulting the nature and purpose of the family unit.

Husbands were separated from wives. Children were separated from their parents. Relatives were torn from one another. The Khmer Rouge decided who would marry whom. Often the bride and groom were complete strangers. Women who resisted state-arranged marriages to strangers were sent off to reeducation camps or executed. Men and women were stripped of their right to choose marriage partners or their right not to marry at all. Marrying was no longer a private affair; it was nationalized. This was an example of Khmer Rouge policy at its most bizarre—*Lord of the Flies* taking a sharp turn and entering into the realm of Huxley's *Brave New World* and Atwood's *The Handmaid's Tale*.

Women who refused sexual relations inside a forced marriage were beaten, and if they persisted, they were taken away for summary execution. In one example, a woman who had refused sexual relations after the forced marriage was stripped naked by the Khmer Rouge cadre and her "husband" was required to consummate the marriage in front of them. Khmer Rouge would go around to rough shelters where couples lived and spy on them to determine whether they were having sex.

The purpose of the Khmer Rouge policy was to breed a new generation of ethnically pure Khmer who would be indoctrinated in the ideology of the Khmer Rouge. Forced marriages were part of a series of radical ideological based racial policies designed to create a new society. Six hundred fifty of the 3,800 registered civilian victims in the trial were victims of forced marriages.

Marriage and family have always been central to Cambodian culture and village life. In ancient times a prospective husband would be required to live with the prospective wife's family for three years. During that time he would be integrated into the family, or if the effort failed, he was sent packing. Today, Khmer weddings are lavish three-day celebrations. As elsewhere in Southeast Asia, Cambodian culture is conservative about marriage, virginity and rape. None of those values survived during the years of the Khmer Rouge forced marriage policy. Marriages were arranged between two strangers with as little as one or two hours' notice.

The Khmer Rouge was obsessed by an ideology of racial purity. The genocide against the Cham and the Vietnamese, also part of Case 2, is another example of the desire to breed and maintain a racially pure Khmer population and exterminate those who were "impure." If the husband was Khmer and the wife Cham, the husband would be spared but his wife and children would be executed. Why the children, who were half Khmer? On the theory that they suckled milk from an impure mother. And should the husband/father show sadness or remorse, he would be liable to execution as well.

The Khmer Rouge embraced the idea of the "blank slate" and believed that if they could reset society from year zero, they could write a new vision of life onto the minds of the generation they had created. That blank slate had to be a Khmer one. All other ethnic groups were excluded.

Such policies raise the question of what psychological damage from childhood abuse or neglect might explain the Khmer Rouge leadership's attitudes toward women, marriage and family? What combination of personal childhood pain and Marxist ideology was responsible for a policy designed to destroy the traditional family? During the course of the trial, perhaps some evidence will indicate what lay in the background of the accused that convinced them to institute policies that violated every cultural norm, every ethical value, and the very network of relatives and family that any ordinary Cambodian would have experienced as a child.

The Failure of Empathy

The crimes outlined on opening day point to a consistent conclusion: the failure of empathy on the part of the leaders meant there was no longer any constraining emotional counterforce to limit how one human being treated another. The ideology of the Khmer Rouge leadership blocked the most natural of human impulses—for persons to place themselves in the situation of another and to experience that person's emotions as if they were their own. Scientists such as Frans de Waal support the idea that empathy is innate. All of us are born with mirror neurons. These neurons trigger an emotional response when, for example, we witness the suffering or pain of another. When we see a sad person, we instinctively feel their sadness.

The Khmer Rouge found a way to disarm the empathy trigger. A cadre that witnessed another's fear did not seek to reduce it. Those who were the perceived enemies of the state lost their status as human beings and no longer qualified as objects of empathy or sympathy. The other had no purchase over the emotion of the torturer. Or, if there was a slip, and a torturer found himself hesitating, the chances were that he would also be tortured and killed, so there was a strong incentive not to have feelings for others. Those who couldn't turn off that trigger committed suicide or were themselves killed by others who had no problem withholding empathy. It was no surprise to hear the co-prosecutor mention numerous incidents of cannibalism as even the victims facing starvation no longer saw each other as human. There have been reported incidents of Khmer Rouge cadres cutting out the livers of living beings and eating them.

This doesn't make easy reading. We try to avoid such thoughts. They are too repellent. But to deny there was a time in Cambodia when such things regularly happened won't be easy, because the evidence will be made public throughout the weeks and months and years ahead.

One of the things this evidence will establish is that, once the empathy light had been extinguished, anything to consolidate power, expand authority, and suppress opposition became justifiable as policy. Making the other party a demon, an outsider—like germs, filth, excrement—made the next step to purify an easy one, the means being torture and murder. What is instinctively abhorrent for most people became mandatory government policy.

The core idea of such a trial is that no ruler or leader anywhere in the world is permitted to disengage the empathy mechanism and send youths on a rampage throughout the population, slaughtering, torturing and humiliating. No ideology, belief system, enemy (real or perceived) or utopian ideal can justify such policies. A line has been drawn in the sand between what is and what is not politically permissible.

It was ironic that one of Ieng Sary's lawyers, Michael Karnavas, asked the court to allow his client to be removed from the courtroom. His client suffered pain, he said, and would be more comfortable in a room downstairs. The President of the court denied the request. It was a special moment in which one of those who had had no empathy for others was formally asking for compassion from the court. Khieu Samphan's French lawyer, Jacques Verges, again without a hint of irony, requested that judges remember that those on trial were "human beings." These human beings, who had denied that status to as many as two million of their fellow citizens, were now seeking shelter within the embrace of empathy, asking for refuge in the emotion that makes us human—the very emotion their policies sought to eradicate. The next couple of years are bound to be filled with many such moments of irony.

What are the lessons of the opening day? Hopefully, those who witnessed it—who attended in person, watched on TV or listened on the radio—came away with confidence that the story can now be told. It will come out in the open. Those who made the policies are no longer safely tucked behind the walls of their secure villas. They are being held to account. Both the international and Cambodian communities are working together to find a way to mark the legal boundaries of what will be tolerated and what will not. The Animal Farm is being dismantled.

Cambodia, through this trial, is also sharing its new-found rules with the world, setting limits on the power any leader can deploy against his own people or others.

And it is showing the world that if those constraints are exceeded, such leaders can be brought to account for their policies and actions. Given the unrest and suppression in many places around the world, all eyes should be on Cambodia and the ECCC. A small, war-torn country with a tragic history is giving back to the world the most precious of all human things: the hope for a better, safer and more secure future.

At the end of all of this, someone will one day write the narrative account of how such a regime comes about. It will stand as an indictment not just of the Khmer Rouge but also of a generation of leaders around the world who turned the other way when the light of empathy dimmed, flickered and was finally extinguished in Cambodia. Someone will write it down for future generations, so they can remember things that no person should ever forget.

Christopher G. Moore

Christopher G. Moore is a Canadian novelist and essayist who lives in Bangkok. He has written 24 novels, including the award-winning Vincent Calvino series and the Land of Smiles Trilogy. The German edition of his third Vincent Calvino novel, *Zero Hour in Phnom Penh*, won the German Critics Award (Deutsche Krimi Preis) for International Crime Fiction in 2004 and the Spanish edition of the same novel won the Premier Special Director's Book Award Semana Negra (Spain) in 2007. The second Vincent Calvino novel, *Asia Hand,* won the Shamus Award for Best Original Paperback in 2011.

Jai Yen

Colin Cotterill

"Swarthy" was the word that best fit him. With his mop of ebony black hair I could imagine him at the microphone at the Pepsi Karaoke, crooning middle-aged women into bed. But really, who needs a swarthy Buddhist abbot? I would have settled for piously rugged or even serenely upright. "Swarthy" just made you wonder what he'd done to warrant internment in our local temple. In Thailand criminals on the lam are renowned for shaving their heads and hiding out in temples. You'd never be able to pick one out in a lineup.

But Te Win and I had braved the minefield of stray dogs to get to the abbot's hut and interrupted him trimming his eyebrows with a pair of scissors as large as garden sheers. I wondered why he didn't use a razor but didn't see it as my place to ask. He didn't look up from the mirror. He asked us what we wanted and I stated my case in Thai. We were hoping to open a class for Burmese kids, I told him. There were some six thousand Burmese living around our little fishing town, and a few hundred kids were knocking about every day with nothing to do. By the time they reached twelve they were easy pickings for the gangs and the boat agents and the karaoke lounges. Why not? They'd never amount to anything. They'd never been to school. Couldn't even read, the heathens.

"So, sooner than hack our way through the bureaucratic overgrowth of the laity, how about letting us set up a class in one of the empty rooms at the temple?" I asked, although this translation is far more eloquent than I'd managed in my clumsy Thai.

He said yes, too soon. We hadn't even given him any details. We didn't have any details. We'd agreed to play it by ear. See what his reaction would be and then come up with a project proposal. We hadn't been that confident we'd get permission. But then again I didn't have any confidence in his answer either.

"Yes?" I asked.

"Certainly. We've got six buildings doing nothing. Every time the local Buddhist Council gets a donation they build something. Might as well get some use out of them."

Te Win, as usual, had kept quiet. His Thai was better than mine. He'd been in Thailand for twenty-six years and currently worked in a machine shop not far from the harbour. He had to deal with the staccato southern dialect day after day. His early Beatles haircut and handlebar moustache were a sort of homage to the decade when time had stood still in his country, currently known as Myanmar. He was a soft-spoken man who, to his wife's displeasure, spent most of his free time helping people. When we were together he'd usually keep his mouth shut and let me make a fool of myself. He told me that requests would be more kindly received from one of the white colonial overlords than from a Burmese. He'd seen a lot over the years. Suffered from the same racism and corruption and deception that some of the younger arrivals were still experiencing today. He knew the ropes.

We walked together across the vast grounds to a huddle of huts at the back. The dogs tagged behind without enthusiasm.

"So, do you speak Thai?" the abbot asked me.

One gets used to that question after a long conversation one had believed was in Thai.

"I try," I said.

Like a magician he produced a ring of keys from his pocketless robes and opened a door to a spotlessly clean hut with plastic chairs stacked at the far end and a glary whiteboard.

"Here," he said. "Never been used. Never been sure what to do with it. We have a row of rooms for evening classes and a meeting hall and all the religious edifices. So this has been sitting empty for a year."

I noticed then that he'd only managed to trim the one eyebrow. It made it hard to stare him in the face.

"So, when can we start?" Te Win asked.

That was typical. I'd do the stalking and he'd go in for the kill.

"Just as soon as you get permission from the police," he said.

"The police?"

"That's right. They need to know when we have gatherings in case there's a traffic snarl-up. It's quite standard procedure. They have a form you can fill in."

Our Burmese weren't allowed to ride motorcycles or drive cars, so I wasn't sure what kind of traffic mayhem a dozen bicycles might lead to. But, buoyed by the fact that we'd been given a sort of permission, I parked my Mighty X pickup in the yard at the front of the Pak Nam police station and took time to admire the regimented primroses behind their tiny white picket fence. This was a police station with little to do. I was about to be the highlight of their day. Te Win, wary of the police for good reasons, had left this one to me. I climbed the steps and smiled at the desk sergeant in the open-air lobby. He looked around for someone who might speak English. Two younger men lowered their heads and clattered away at their typewriters.

"I need permission for a gathering," I said, in Thai. "The abbot at the temple said you have a form."

He glared at me and, in Thai, asked me if I spoke Thai. One gets used to it.

"He wants a permission form for a gathering," said one of the younger men, as if translating.

"You want a permission form for a gathering?" asked the sergeant.

"Yes," I replied, my smile unwavering.

On the drive over I'd rather hoped he'd have the form in front of him on the desk and I'd just take it home and have someone fill it out. But instead he picked up the phone and told a superior there was a foreigner in the lobby who wanted a permission form for a gathering. He nodded as he listened and then put his hand over the receiver.

"Who's gathering?" he asked.
"Children," I said.
"How many?" he asked.
"About thirty."
"How long's the gathering?"
"Eight till four. Monday to Saturday."
"That's every day."
"Give or take a Sunday."

He passed this information on and nodded sternly as he listened.

At last he said, "This is like a school, right?"

"Yes," I said. "Exactly like it."

"Well, then you don't need a permission form for a gathering," he said. "The school has the right to gather on its own property."

"Ah, but this will be held in the temple," I said.

"Why would children need to go to school in a temple?" he asked. "We've got perfectly good schools in the district."

"These children haven't been accepted by the Thai schools."

"Why not?"

I sat on a small pink plastic chair in front of the major's battleship of a desk. He was a large man whose body seemed to be searching for a way out of his skin-tight brown uniform.

"Burmese?" he said.

"Yes. Children."

"And you are the teacher?"

"No."

"Why not?"

I wondered if he only spoke in questions.

"Because I can't speak Burmese, and the parents want their kids to read and write their own language. We have a Burmese teacher."

"They're here in Thailand. They should study Thai. It's only good manners," he said. "We're the hosts. They should know how to talk to us. Understand when we tell 'em what to do. Don't waste time teaching 'em Burmese. Send 'em to a Thai school."

He made it sound easy. Thailand had ratified the United Nations Convention on the Rights of the Child in 1992 but, like rich children who didn't like beans and squash, the government chose to spit out those portions that weren't to its taste. Into the pedal bin went articles that dealt with nationality and refugee status, leaving the Burmese with very few rights. It did accept that Burmese children had the right to an education and could attend primary school. It did not, however, provide specialized language training or Burmese-speaking teachers. There were no rooms made available for these children, and Thai teachers, already struggling to do their job in large classes, complained bitterly that the foreigners were an unwanted distraction. So, assuming the Burmese parents were prepared and able to go through the confusing registration process, they'd see their children tossed into the mix and told to sort it all out themselves. Thus we come to child's inhumanity to child. The Burmese were bullied mercilessly. Hardly surprising, then, that so few children of day labourers attended school. But this wasn't an argument I expected to win with a police officer.

"If they studied Burmese, they'd all go back there," he continued.

"That's the plan."

"And where would that leave us? All our local industries would come to a halt. The fisheries, the palm oil, construction, tourism. There'd be no labourers."

Teaching children Burmese wasn't going to stop that from happening. As soon as they thought they'd be able to earn a living wage in their home country, the workers would be off. With Auntie Aung San Suu Kyi in there shaking things up, that might not have been such a distant dream. None of the migrants enjoyed the indignity of being pool boys to the Thais. But, again, I wasn't there to argue. He looked down at the permission form for a gathering that lay on the desk in front of him. His half-lens glasses made him look like a sunburned version of Ebenezer Scrooge. He needed motivation.

"I hear you have problems with some of the Burmese kids," I said.

"We do that."

"So, wouldn't it be a good idea to round them up off the streets so they aren't stealing from shops or pickpocketing?" (There was no evidence that Burmese children committed these acts, but the rumours had become suburban legend.) "If they were all in one place, you'd know where to go to interview them."

He looked up and squinted.

"It's not a bad idea," he said.

"The benefits are endless," I agreed.

"But I can't sign it."

"Why not?"

"Because they're Burmese. A gathering of foreign nationals isn't an issue for the Royal Thai Police. It's a security matter."

"They're under eleven."

"That's irrelevant. You're in the wrong place. You should be talking to the military. You get permission from them, and I'll see what I can do about signing this form."

My cup of tea arrived just as I was leaving.

Although it's hard to hold them down long enough to count them, Burmese workers in Thailand, according to conservative estimates, are estimated to number over two million. That's eighty percent of the migrant worker force. It was true that much of the kingdom's industry relied on Burmese labour and that a large-scale repatriation would bankrupt the place. It was hardly surprising, therefore, that before he went into exile, Prime Minister Thaksin Shinawatra adopted a program of registering these migrants rather than rounding them up and shipping them home. Few Burmese trusted this new initiative, and still only half a million workers were registered. The rest remained open to shady employment practices and abuse. Many were shifted here and there by agents who scooped a good helping off their salaries. The two hundred thousand or so children who traveled with them rarely saw the inside of a school. But Thailand's 2005 announcement of an "Education for All" policy looked really good on the advertising hoardings.

I'm allergic to telephones, so I let my wife call the Defense Ministry to inquire about the hoops one needed to jump through to get kids into a classroom. Just to be sure, I persuaded Te Win to remove bomb-making, weapons training and insurgency from the curriculum. Play dough would inevitably lead to Semtex, so we left out art and craft as well.

My wife had been referred to the department of Home Security and was talking to a colonel. She began by writing down the instructions he gave but stopped after the tenth item. Now she was just smiling and saying *ka* a lot. From time to time I'd hear, "But they're only children"—which apparently had no effect. When it was all over, she turned off the phone, scrunched the sheet of paper into a ball and found the litter bin from four yards.

"That hopeless?" I asked.

"They want a background check on the parents and photographs of all the kids."

"It doesn't seem real. They're children."

"I must have forgotten to mention that."

"Any hints as to how we might avoid military retribution?"

"Only one. He said if it's a government-instigated proposal, we wouldn't have to submit the application directly to the military. They have channels."

"The government? Great. Give me the phone and I'll call the PM."

"It could be a grassroots project, suggested by the community, submitted by the town hall."

Most of the kids around Pak Nam were the children of families working in the fishing industry. Many of the wives would work in the packing or processing factories while the husbands went out for two or three nights at a time to catch fish. But most of the fishing boat crews were single men, most of them trafficked illegally from Ranong. Some with debts to their "agents" that would take months to repay. Slavery and imprisonment were common and well-documented.

During the down periods when fishing was restricted to allow the fish to spawn, the Burmese would be fed but not paid. There was a similar policy with those working on the drying benches where sand fish and squid were sunbaked. No sun, no pay. With the transient nature of the work, there was no coordination of workers, no union, no organized body to make formal complaints. The few NGOs working with migrant labourers had their hands full just keeping up, and smaller towns like ours weren't represented at all. It surprised me, given this lack of coordination, that the military might consider the Burmese a threat to Thai national security. But, I guessed, the army didn't really have that much to keep them entertained. Sudoku only went so far.

Jai Yen

The *tesaban* (municipal) office was too small for all the tasks that had been assigned to it. People of every hue and scent sat side by side on wooden benches, clutching the squares of paper on which were written their queue numbers. I fondly recalled my early days in Thailand before the concept of queuing had been imported— probably from England. Back then, a maul of hot people would crowd around the official's desk, elbowing themselves into his line of sight. This new etiquette felt uncomfortably civilized. Te Win and I had explained our query to the woman at the door whose only purpose seemed to be the handing out of pink, yellow or blue queue squares. I'd thought she might give us a fast-track white square to take us directly to the mayoress, but like the octogenarian betel gnawer to our left and the fishy lady in red Wellington boots to our right, we had a yellow square, which appeared to mean "other."

After half an hour our number came up, and we found ourselves sitting in front of an attractive young lady who couldn't have been much older then twelve. Her uniform fit her like a dress-up. She looked up from her stack of papers and said, "Oh!" the way the cinematic heroin might awaken to find Frankenstein leaning over the bed. She blushed and turned to her colleagues.

"Anyone here speak English?" she shouted.

There was no reply.

"Only me by the sound of it," I said, in Thai.

"Do you speak Thai?" she asked slowly, ignoring Te Win entirely.

One gets used to it.

"I try," I smiled.

She returned my smile with relief and we became friends. She could not, however, help us with our plight.

"You should go up and speak to Uncle Sumit," she said.

"We should?"

"He's the director of grassroots projects."

Sounds like exactly the man we should have been speaking to forty minutes ago, I thought, but kept it to myself. One learns not to antagonize public officials because, inevitably, one will find oneself beamed back into that same chair at a future date when a sympathetic clerk could make life so much easier.

Uncle Sumit had an office the size of a toilet cubicle on the upper floor. His position, Director of Grassroots Projects, was stenciled above the door. The paint had dribbled a little from some of the characters. There was only room for one guest, so I wrestled Te Win onto the chair and stood behind. Sumit was a lively old man with a bulge of talismans under his shirt and a wispy white moustache that didn't join up in the middle. He listened attentively, smiled warmly and nodded as if his head were joined to his shoulders on a bedspring. As I talked, he threw in a "good," in English here and there. He did not, surprisingly, ask us if we spoke Thai.

"It's a marvelous idea," he said when we finished our pitch.

"You think so?" Te Win asked.

"Certainly. Low budget. Huge influence. It's exactly what we've been talking about to bring us a bit closer to the Burmese community. You'll be off home soon enough if we don't start showing you lot some respect. We've been proposing some community projects for the Burmese. I do think there'll be a football match later in the year."

Yes, I thought. A football match should make life more tolerable.

"I don't think there'll be any problem at all," Uncle Sumit concluded.

"Really?"

Te Win and I had spoken at the same time. We'd become a little skeptical since we'd started our trail of enthusiastic rejections.

"So, when can we start?" Te Win asked.

"Right now. Right now."

He swiveled round on his wheelie chair and reached into a metal cabinet. He pulled out a foolscap file with a blue plastic spine. It was some hundred pages thick and was the Grassroots Project application form.

"It looks daunting," he said, "but I can go through it with you."

"And where does it go from here?" I asked.

"To the budget committee for its annual meeting."

"Annual, meaning …?"

"Every year."

"I got that. I was just wondering when the committee meeting would be."

"End of the fiscal year."

"That's September."

"Correct."

"This is February. That's seven months off."

"In fact it will be more like nineteen months 'cause we already have our quota of proposals for next year."

"Nineteen months? The kids will have all grown up and married by then," I said.

He laughed like a man who truly enjoyed laughing.

"*Jai yen*," he said.

How I hated that expression. Whenever we foreigners showed even the slightest urgency it would be considered a weakness caused by the heat of our emotions. "*Jai yen*" was an instruction to keep our hearts cool. So, as we had little choice, urged by my Burmese friend, I put out the fire in my ribcage with several deep breaths and started to trudge through that endless document that might one day deep in the future allow us to give a small group of children the opportunity that was theirs by right. By page seven my heart was giving off steam again.

"Uncle," I said, "you live here and you understand rural life. And you know the ways of bureaucracy. Surely there's a shortcut to get around all this red tape without breaking any laws?"

He pursed his lips and looked towards the open doorway. When he spoke, it was in a whisper.

"You know, there is a way," he said.

"There is?"

"There's an autonomous body in Thailand that can set up its own projects without asking for government approval."

"Excellent. Who are they?"

"The Supreme Sangha Buddhist Council. That might save you a bit of time and effort. You should go and have a word with the abbot. I hear they've got rooms available."

Two weeks later, still dizzy, having stepped off the roundabout while it was still spinning, Te Win rented a room in the old ice works, decorated it and made Lilliputian furniture. He interviewed a few people who had graduated from universities and colleges and were now gutting mackerel. He found a teacher with experience and arranged the loan of her from the ice factory. Twenty-two children arrived on the first day, increasing to forty when word got out that it wasn't a trap by the government to kidnap migrants and deport them. Paranoia has a sound basis for the Burmese. I arranged for books to be sent by friends in Yangon and cleared the stationery shelf at Tesco.

We opened our school fully expecting to get into trouble. We didn't have permission from the police, the military or the town hall. We just did it. Unannounced people in various shades of uniform have stopped by, stood in the doorway, nodded, smiled a little. But three years down the track it's still going strong. That's it, you see? By asking permission, you bump up against people whose job it is not to give it. There's a sigh of relief when you just go ahead and do it.

One gets used to it.

Colin Cotterill

Colin Cotterill is a London-born teacher, crime writer and cartoonist. He currently lives in Southeast Asia, where he writes the award-winning Dr. Siri Paiboun mystery series set in the People's Democratic Republic of Laos, and the Jimm Juree crime novels set in southern Thailand.

The second novel in his Dr. Siri series, *Thirty Three Teeth*, won the Dilys Award in 2006, and the French edition of the first novel in the series, *Le Dejeuner du Coroner (The Coroner's Lunch)*, won the Prix SNCF Du Polar in 2007. The Dr. Siri Series won the CWA Dagger in The Library Award for Colin in 2009. In 2010 the seventh Dr. Siri novel, *Love Songs from a Shallow Grave*, was a finalist for the Dilys Award.

Transformation

Barbara Nadel

I can't remember exactly when the incident I'm about to relate happened. All I know is that it occurred before İstanbul's main shopping street, İstiklal Caddesi, was pedestrianized. This probably places it at sometime in the late 1980s, when İstiklal was still a traffic-choked hymn to carbon monoxide instead of the airy, walkable space it is today.

It was night-time and I was making my way towards the Tünel funicular railway after a boozy night out with friends. As ever, İstiklal was stiff with traffic as well as with badly parked cars at the side of the road. As I walked past one of these cars, a large Mercedes Benz, I noticed a very attractive man leaning out of the window talking to a very tall blonde woman. I didn't think anything of it until I heard shouting.

Initially I thought that the man was trying to drag the woman into his car against her will. But then I saw that he was actually out of the car and was wrestling with her on the pavement. Many of us passersby stopped to gawp. We all saw the man slap the handcuffs on the woman at about the same moment. We also all saw another man pull the woman's wig off. At a conservative estimate the transsexual who had just been arrested for soliciting was two metres tall. As far as my fellow revellers and I were concerned, she was also the victim of an act of police entrapment.

This is the sort of incident that could cause one to arrive at the conclusion that transgendered people were *personae non gratae* in 1980s Turkey. One might be forgiven for thinking that this is still the case today. But because we are talking about Turkey, this is not a straightforward issue. The old cliché about a country that bridges too continents is not always a hackneyed and pointless observation. Although I would argue that both European and Asian attitudes cannot just simply be categorized in terms of European = liberal, Asian = conservative, there is something in the idea that Turks can and do live with and accept competing values. There is a saying amongst Turks, and also amongst expats in Turkey, which is used to explain everything that they don't understand about the country. It goes (accompanied by a shrug), "This is Turkey." And this applies to transgendered people in spades.

İstanbul in particular has always been a magnet for people who want to live alternative lifestyles. Big cities in general draw those who want to express themselves in ways that may be considered outlandish or unacceptable in the countryside. But with regard to cross-dressing or cross-gendering, İstanbul has a particularly long history.

As early as the fifth century AD, reports of transvestite nuns in the convents of Byzantium were recorded. St. Mary, also called Marinos, followed her father into a monastery. After his death Mary/Marinos was accused of "fathering" a child herself, which she did not deny, and indeed she brought the infant up in the monastery as her own. Only after her death was her true gender discovered. Later her life was deemed holy enough to warrant canonization, as was the life of St. Anastasia Patrikia, who fled the advances of the Byzantine emperor Justinian to live in the Egyptian desert as the monk Anastasios. In the case of the latter divine, one can argue that there was compulsion to adopt a male guise. But St. Mary's cross-dressing was a choice, and it was, and is, one that is recognized and revered in the Eastern Orthodox Church.

Of course modern Turkey is a majority Muslim society which, prior to becoming a republic in 1923, was the Ottoman Turkish Empire. This vast and diverse entity encompassed most of the modern Middle East, the Balkans, Greece, and parts of Eastern Europe. While mindful of Islamic rules regarding the seclusion of women and "good" women's chastity, Ottoman society tolerated not only female prostitution but also cross-dressing male dancers/prostitutes known as *kocekler* or *zenne*. Generally recruited from the empire's subject races— Greeks, Armenians, Albanians, Roma—the *kocekler* were employed both inside and outside the Ottoman court until the beginning of the twentieth century, when the empire collapsed. *Kocekler* would dance at weddings, festivals and circumcision celebrations. Sexually available men would frequently fight for their favours, which were always of a passive, "feminine" nature. Even today mainstream Turkish society still makes great play of the difference between "active" and "passive" homosexual acts. Only the passive partner is regarded as being truly homosexual; the active partner retains his heterosexual "manhood." This is most graphically illustrated by punishments meted out by the military to servicemen caught in the act of sexual congress. The passive partner will be dishonourably discharged, while the active partner will be punished but retain his place within his chosen service.

There has never been and still is not any actual law against homosexuality, lesbianism, bisexuality, cross-dressing or transgendered people either in the Ottoman Empire or in the Republic of Turkey. However, things did change for cross-dressing entertainers in the wake of the military putsch of 1981. To return Turkey to the kind of military "purity" that, as they saw it, had swept away the old empire and created a new, modern republic, the generals who ruled the country at that time cracked down on trans people, banning them from cities and dumping them in forests with no money, food or means of support. They also placed a ban on male-to-female cross-dressing entertainers. This negatively affected two huge singing stars at the time: Zeki Müren (1931–96) and Bülent Ersoy (1952–).

Müren, though flamboyant in the style of Liberace and openly gay, could just about manage to get past this new law, but Ersoy could not. Cross-dressing was such a large part of his act that he eventually had gender reassignment surgery. Afterwards, Bülent Ersoy was very influential in a successful campaign to add a new article to the civil code in 1988 which allowed transgendered people to have their birth certificates and ID cards altered in line with their new identities. However, in 2002 new preconditions were formulated for those wishing to have gender reassignment in Turkey, which included the necessity of such people being "unproductive." This meant and means unable to produce children. So to obtain gender reassignment surgery in Turkey, one has to basically destroy one's procreative ability first, either by drugs or surgery or a combination of the two. The law is also clearly problematic when it comes to people who wish to obtain gender reassignment surgery *after* the production of children. However, it is not just the law that is difficult for transgendered people in Turkey; it is also the attitudes, opinions and habits of some of their fellow citizens. In spite of its long history of cross-dressing people in its midst, Turkish society is not always at ease with this phenomenon.

In Turkey the story of modern, organized lesbian, gay, bisexual and transgendered (LGBT) movements started in 1993 with the founding of Lambda İstanbul. Initially formed as a reaction against the police banning of a parade to commemorate Christopher Street Day (when the Stonewall Riots and hence the Gay Liberation Movement started in the United States in 1969), it has become a pressure group as well as an information centre. Allied to sister organizations in Ankara (KAOS GL—gay, and Sappho'nun Kizlari—lesbian), Lambda provides sexual health advice, support and a social context for lesbian, gay, bisexual and trans people all over the country. It also presents an annual prize, called the Genetically Modified Tomato Award, for the most homo/trans-phobic speech or action of the year. This award gets its rather unusual name from a statement issued by Turkish footballer Erman Torogulu that eating genetically modified food would turn people gay.

Risible though Torogulu's statement was, his fears about and distrust of gay, lesbian and trans people did reflect a view within society that almost led to the disbanding of Lambda in 2008. A complaint against Lambda for acting "against the law and morality" by the İstanbul Governor's Office was upheld by the Third Court of First Instance in the Beyoğlu district of İstanbul. The case had started back in 2007 when the Governor's

Office had complained that Lambda, just by existing, was acting against Turkish morals and family values. In April 2008 the police raided Lambda's offices, seizing literature that allegedly "encouraged" prostitution. It looked as if Lambda was doomed.

However, in November 2008 Lambda took its case to the Supreme Court of Appeals in Ankara, which overturned the Third Court of First Instance's decision. This decision was based upon the right that LGBT people have to form associations. It also recognized that the existence of Lambda was not a threat to the family or to the moral values of the country. The İstanbul court then reversed its decision and Lambda reopened in 2009. It remains open now.

Around İstanbul's central Taksim Square, and especially in the area bisected by İstanbul Caddesi, there are a lot of clubs, bars and cafés that are LGBT friendly. Rainbow flags can be seen outside many of the establishments, and bookshops in the area sell guides to İstanbul that include sections for LGBT people as well as literature that includes queer content. There are websites that offer help and information to LGBT tourists to the city, and this year, 2012, will mark the tenth anniversary of İstanbul's annual gay pride festivities.

But problems remain, some of which were exemplified in last year's pride march in İstanbul. Thousands took to the streets, including deputies from the BDP, the pro-Kurdish Peace and Democracy Party, who support LGBT rights. It was a peaceful but determined march which had at its core demands for three basic things:

> 1) the addition of a clause related to "sexual orientation and identity" into existing anti-discrimination laws,

2) union rights for sex workers and
3) the development of hate-crime legislation.

On a more general level the marchers also called for social recognition of LGBT people and stronger police action on crimes against them. That said, the marchers were not impeded, attacked or hampered, and the day concluded without incident—a marvellous example of "This is Turkey," where certain situations are and are not as they seem. A lot depends upon whom you speak to.

Since 2002 Turkey has been governed by the Adalet ve Kalkinma Partisi (AKP or AK Party)—in English, the Justice and Development Party. Formed in 2001, the AKP is a centre-right conservative party that is pro-Western and is in the process of preparing for accession to the European Union. To do this, the AKP have worked hard to bring aspects of Turkish law and police practice in line with EU standards. AK advocates a liberal market economy and has made some headway in improving relations with some of Turkey's minorities (Armenian, Greek, Jewish, Syriac). It has been in power for three terms.

However, depending upon whom you speak to and how you interpret certain events that the current government has been involved with, all may not be as straightforward as it seems. AK was originally formed from a wide range of politicians with an equally wide range of views. Nevertheless, the core of the party, including the current prime minister, Recep Tayyip Erdogan, and the president, Abdullah Gul, came originally from the reformist wing of an Islamist party called the Virtue Party.

Turkey has been a secular republic since 1923. Enshrined in legislation laid down by the founder of the republic, Mustafa Kemal Atatürk, the country has been ruled by leaders, often backed by the military, who support that notion without question. AK say that they support the secular republic too, but because of their past—the fact that Erdogan, Gul and others are openly religious—and because of what some people interpret as the moralistic tone of their legislation, not everyone believes them. During their time in office, AK have sought, without success, to criminalize adultery (or, rather, recriminalize it—adultery had been a criminal offence under the secular administration of the early 1990s), have extended the number of Imam Hatip religious schools in the country, and have imprisoned several ex-generals and political opponents on, depending again upon whom you speak to, either legitimate or illegitimate charges of treason. AK say that these individuals have, in the past, planned to overthrow the democratically elected government—a very serious charge. However, until these people are brought to trial and evidence is formally presented, it is hard to make an informed judgement on this issue either way.

Dyed-in-the-wool secularists point towards everything and anything that AK does as evidence of its "real" mission to "Islamicize" Turkey. Whether their fears are well-founded or not is beyond the scope of this essay, which only includes this information as background to the central subject of transgendered people in Turkey. As far as trans people are concerned, there are multiple social problems to be faced if they are to achieve full equality in Turkey, and not all of them revolve around religious conservatism.

That said, there is no denying that a new, more socially conservative elite has developed under AK, and this has led to things like widespread fasting during Ramazan and the wearing of headscarves by women becoming more visible within Turkish society. Those who value such things actually feel freer than they have ever done before. Alongside conservative phenomena like the above, legislation to bring Turkey in line with leading states within the EU has also had an effect upon social norms. In 2009, as in France, Germany and the UK, smoking was banned in enclosed public places in Turkey. In a country with a very long and ingrained tradition of smoking, where puffing on water pipes (*nargile*) is still common practice, this was contentious, and a lot of people opposed to the ban blamed the AK government and particularly the Prime Minister, who is known to abhor the habit. However, the reality is that the smoking ban had actually been in force on public transport and in cinemas for some years with no problems. Smoke-free restaurants and cafés were merely an extension of what already existed as a public health initiative.

Actually more worrying for secular Turks is the government's attitude towards alcohol. Government-run restaurants which used to serve it now don't, and in one part of the central Beyoğlu area of the city, pavement tables have been removed outside drinking establishments and restaurants. The official line is that local residents were complaining about the noise, but some people interpret the removal of the tables as a moral judgement about drinking and smoking outside.

Whatever the truth about governmental motives might be, what is difficult to deny is that a growing societal conservatism and a nationalistic militarism, which remains a force within the country, can and do have an impact, not always a positive one, upon the lives of transgendered people in Turkey. Trans people negotiate their existences within what can be perceived as a triangle between the forces of nationalistic militarism, moral conservatism and a natural ease with cross-dressing and shifting gender identities that has always existed, especially in cities like İstanbul. But how does all this theorizing translate into the real lives of transsexual people living and working in Turkey?

On October 7, 2011, the *Hurriyet Daily News*, a Turkish newspaper, reported that a trans woman called Ramazan Çetin had been murdered by her brother in the eastern city of Gaziantep. He'd shot her three times, once through the head, to "cleanse" his "honour." Brother and killer Fevzi Çetin is reported to have told the police who arrested him, "My brother was engaged in transvestism, I killed him."

Gaziantep is a traditional eastern Turkish city and is in no way the magnet for "difference" that İstanbul is. But then, across Turkey in the previous year, 2010, sixteen people had been killed because of their perceived sexual orientation or preference, and this included victims in the city of İstanbul. Ramazan Çetin's death was not and is not an isolated case. A survey of 104 transsexual women in İstanbul conducted by Lambda in 2011 revealed that eighty-nine percent of those polled had been subjected to violence whilst in police custody. It can be argued that such violence is not unusual wherever you live in the world and whatever your sexual orientation. But the fact is that transgendered women in İstanbul find themselves in police cells more often than most other people because most of them work as prostitutes. This is not a choice so much as a necessity as trans people find it hard to persuade mainstream employers to give them jobs. However, prostitution is legal in Turkey, and so the question arises as to why these girls are getting arrested by the police.

As has been stated before, there are no laws against LGBT people in Turkey. There is nothing. Prostitution is officially legal (since 1923), and so it is reasonable to ask where the police might come into this picture. The reality is that not all prostitutes work legally in Turkey.

Legal prostitutes are required to be registered with their names recorded by the police. They are issued ID cards listing the health checks and examinations they are obliged to have by law. In the past most prostitutes working in Turkey were registered local girls, many of whom worked for the famous İstanbul madam Matild Manukyan in one of her thirty-two licensed brothels. But when Matild died in 2001, her son sold all her properties and businesses, and since that time things have changed a lot in the world of Turkish prostitution. In an effort to discourage prostitution the government has been quietly closing official brothels since 2002. Licenses for new women wishing to become registered prostitutes have not been granted, and there are now an estimated 30,000 women on waiting lists all over the country. These days unregistered prostitutes far and away outnumber their registered sisters. They are not protected by the law and they include amongst their numbers all the transsexual girls who work out of illegal brothels and/or walk the streets. And of course for the trans women other job opportunities are very hard to come by. Arrest and detention, often accompanied by violence, have therefore become "normal" aspects of transsexual life.

Since the beginning of the twentieth century, there hasn't been what could be described as a "golden" age for trans people in Turkey. But throughout the late 1980s and 1990s the desire to protest about institutional prejudice and to force successive governments to listen grew. One of the most influential of these activists, still very vocal about trans issues today, is Demet Demir (1961–).

In spite of continued oppressive practices from the police as well as, sometimes, prejudice from individuals, in 1985 a considerable number of trans women banded together to rent apartments in a district of İstanbul called Cihangir. Rudely referred to by some as "Faggot Land," this area became famous for its brothels and for the practice (in which some of the girls indulged) of calling out to customers from their windows. Demet was one of those who lived in Cihangir and who was in the district when the police finally moved in to evict the women. Local registered, non-trans brothel keepers had complained to the police about the fact that the trans women were "stealing" their customers. The reality was that they just didn't like the competition. Demet and the other girls moved on to a street called Ulker Sokak, where they set up business again. But prejudice and violence followed them, and by 1989 Ulker Sokak was all but finished.

However, one person refused to leave. In spite of threats from the then local police chief (Beyoğlu district), in spite of attempted breaks-ins by the authorities, in spite of having her electricity cut off and her telephone cables cut and being snubbed by local shopkeepers, Demet stayed, and eventually she was joined by other girls. Today Ulker Sokak is a small but significant area of transgendered activity in the heart of İstanbul.

On June 19, 2011, the second-ever Trans Pride March was held on İstiklal Caddesi, right at the centre of İstanbul's old diplomatic quarter. It was big, loud, proud and colourful and was very well-attended by trans people, lesbians, gays, bisexuals and their supporters from all over the country. And as Demet Demir herself accepts, actions against trans people by the police these days are not usually as serious as they were back in the 1980s. Then a transgendered person could be held in a police cell or made to have humiliating STD tests at a local hospital for days or even weeks on end. These days if a trans person is arrested, she is usually released after a few hours. Although that is still not ideal, it is an improvement. But then the essence of the story of transgendered life in Turkey is one of hard-won gains weighed against the continuing problem of entrenched negative practices and attitudes in society.

In March 2012 a social justice and art project by Gabrielle Le Roux called AI Turkey was published on YouTube. Supported by Amnesty International and the Consulate General of the Netherlands, it consists of a series of films illustrating aspects of transgendered life in Turkey. Transgendered women including Demet Demir and a few transgendered men talk about their lives and experiences in twenty-first-century Turkey. Certain themes across this series of interviews are common to almost all those who took part.

Most of the women are employed in the sex industry, and so much of their work is done at night. Overwhelmingly they fear, not for themselves, but for their friends. Attacks on trans people remain common, and the women see themselves very much as a family that is under threat. Therefore an attack on one is an attack on all, and the worst thing that most of the women can imagine is losing a friend. They recount stories of beatings, rapes and killings, and of judges using the fact of a trans woman's gender as an excuse for limiting the prison sentence of the man who murdered her. Judges who do this say that the victim's gender constitutes an "extenuating circumstance," partially exonerating the offender's behaviour.

Allied to this is the issue of rights in general and the fact that trans people are very aware of the problems that being overlooked by official legislation can bring. While existing in fact, their legislative existence is far more tenuous, and most of them work in a sector of the sex industry that is unregulated and illegal. Their lives are therefore criminalized, which puts them in the same category with people who have criminal records for theft, rape, etc. They want equality before the law but, as the Le Roux interviews illustrate so well, a lot of trans people have an interest in the rights of others, too. Women's, animals' and children's rights are mentioned frequently, and many of the interviewees describe themselves as political activists working (usually in a voluntary capacity) for LGBT organizations like Lambda or Pembe Hayat (Pink Life), an organization that works specifically with transsexual people.

One of the possible ways forward that transsexual people in Turkey see for their rights is via a new constitution. At present the Constitution of the Republic of Turkey guarantees equality before the law for all its citizens. However, no provision is made for the specific needs of particular groups. This is best exemplified in an exchange between a member of parliament for the Democratic Society Party and the then Minister of Justice back in 2008. When asked whether the prevention of discrimination based on sexual orientation should be a principal area of concern for the Justice Ministry, the Minister replied, "since we see all people equal before the law, we don't believe in the necessity of working on specific groups." This can of course be interpreted in a positive way but also in a negative fashion. Turkish law is also not, as yet, in line with those of EU countries like the Netherlands and the UK, which do have legislation specifically protecting LGBT people. It is the opinion of Senem Doganoglu, a lawyer who works pro bono for human rights organizations including Pembe Hayat, that the legislative and judicial authorities in Turkey are accustomed to using criminal sanctions to protect the majority. So while everyone is "equal before the law," the interests of some are traditionally elevated above those of certain others.

Religion and/or spirituality is important to a lot of transsexual people in Turkey. Though some have been brought up in secular, Kemalist households, many come from religious, mainly Islamic, backgrounds. And where faith was important in their families, in spite of religion sometimes being used by their opponents as a "stick" with which to beat them, many transsexuals retain their beliefs. It is also interesting to note how those who do still believe do not criticize Islam or any other religion but rather those people who use faith, as they see it, to persecute others.

Trans life stories can be sad. Some women have been imprisoned in their family homes so that no one outside the family can see them. Others have been beaten by their families, thrown into the street or made to move from one place to another because of fear and prejudice. But some families do accept a trans son or daughter and go to great lengths to protect and assist them. "This is Turkey" is never more visible here than when, even in small villages, families and friends behave against social norms and support those in transition. But even if a family is supportive, work is still an issue and, with a few notable exceptions, most trans people are employed as sex workers. This is not a job any of them seem to enjoy, but it is well-paid, and all of Le Roux's interviewees who were sex workers felt that they earned their money. They also, in common with most people involved in prostitution, saw their working lives on the streets as being hard and short. When men want sex, particularly if they are paying, it is usually with a young woman.

However, in spite of all the negatives that were expressed in the interviews, one big positive point did come across strongly, and that was the growing power of the transsexual lobby.

Trans power is not just growing because of organizations like Lambda and Pembe Hayat or even via events like Trans Pride. All of these things help, but at the core of transsexual liberation in Turkey are the individuals who make up the trans community and who refuse to be silenced.

As well as Demet Demir, Lambda and Pembe Hayat activists—not forgetting megastars like Bülent Ersoy—transsexuals are pushing out and making themselves more visible. Although she was not actually selected to stand for parliament, Oyku Ozen, a transsexual woman from Bursa, applied to stand for the main opposition Republican People's Party (CHP) in 2011. In part Ozen was encouraged to make her bid in the wake of the furious reaction by CHP deputy Mehmet Sevigen to then State Minister for Women and Family Aliye Kavaf, who described homosexuality as "a disease" (2011). Ozen, although unsuccessful herself, opened the debate when she asked the question, "Why can't a transsexual woman be a candidate?" Why not indeed?

The elections of 2011, which Ozen had wanted to stand in, resulted in another victory for the AK Party. On the one hand this seemed to underwrite conservative values that could be injurious to LGBT aspirations for the future. But again, "This is Turkey" came to the fore. In September 2011 AK Party member and Minister for Family and Social Policy Fatma Sahin met with LGBT organizations with a view to working towards including them in the draft of a new national constitution. Then in January 2012 a journalist called Serdar Arseven, a columnist on an Islamic newspaper called *Yeni Akit*, wrote an article that described LGBT people as "perverts." While some people agreed with his assessment, significantly, the Supreme Court of Appeals in Ankara did not, and both Mr. Arseven and his newspaper were fined on the basis that he had used the rhetoric of hate in his argument.

Although not everyone would want to live next door to her, most Turks enjoy listening to Bülent Ersoy and watching her on television. The "acceptable" entertainer image of trans people in Turkey is not at issue. Another hopeful sign is the huge popularity of a film called *Zenne* (2012). Inspired, in part, by what has been described as Turkey's first gay honour killing back in 2008 (gay man Ahmet Yıldız was killed, it is believed, by his father), it tells the story of a fictional relationship between Yıldız and a *zenne* (cross-dressing) dancer. Although initially released only on the film festival circuit, *Zenne* is now in mainstream cinemas all over the country.

And yet Pembe Hayat reports that two trans women died and one was hospitalized (after being shot by a policeman) just in March and April of 2012. All three women were sex workers. The two who died were killed by clients, while the one shot by a policeman was apparently resisting arrest. "This is Turkey" doesn't really do justice to the pain still suffered by trans people, and it certainly doesn't adequately explain it.

However, even if separate legislation like that employed in EU countries were to be brought to bear, would things actually change that much for transgendered people? Back in 2003 I had to help a transsexual woman move out of her flat in a large town in southern England. I was working in mental health services at the time, and the woman was being driven literally "mad" by the prejudicial actions of her neighbours. And while the local police didn't beat her up, they did almost as much damage by ignoring her complaints and not going out to her when she was being attacked. The more you work with the public anywhere in the world, the more you come to realize that some human beings hate difference and enjoy being cruel. In addition the pack mentality is alive and, sadly, very well everywhere.

In Turkey today, certain facts—that organizations like Pembe Hayat exist, that trans people can even contemplate going into government and that even very cautious critics like the writer Elif Safak (in her *Guardian* article of January 18, 2012, "From homophobia to a moving apology in Turkey") feel that things are finally changing—have to be good signs. Personally, I just wish that the change had come in time for the trans woman I saw being arrested all those years ago, back in the late 1980s.

Barbara Nadel

Barbara Nadel is the author of the critically acclaimed detective series featuring Turkish sleuth, Inspector Cetin Ikmen. In 2005 her seventh Ikmen book won the CWA Silver Dagger for Fiction. Whilst continuing with the Ikmen series, Barbara has recently embarked on a new series set in her native East London. The first book, *A Private Business*, was published in July 2012. Her website is www.nadel.co.uk.

Emerging from the Crash

Quentin Bates

This is a young country that has had to grow up quickly. Not much more than half a century ago, Iceland was a rocky outcrop in the middle of the North Atlantic where farmers and fishermen fought to make a living in a country where not much grows. This is a country that grows sheep, grass for hay to keep animals alive through the long winter, a few potatoes and not much else, though it does have some of the Atlantic's most fertile fishing grounds on its doorstep.

Further back in history lies a rich heritage that began in the settlements of ninth-century Norse outcasts who sailed from Norway to escape what they saw as a repressive regime. Arriving in Iceland, they slaughtered or made slaves of the few people they found there ahead of them, probably people who came from Ireland or Scotland to eke out a precarious living by fishing and farming. History has always been written by the victors, and those original inhabitants were never written into the ancient Icelandic sagas, leaving nothing but the most tantalisingly faint clues to their existence.

The Norse newcomers made themselves chieftains, dealing out land to their followers and presiding over an experimental form of government that was perhaps the closest thing the world had seen to democracy since the Athenian state a millennium earlier. It didn't last.

The island became isolated from its neighbours in Norway and Britain. Settlers who had moved on to Greenland and, briefly, North America were unable to survive there. Iceland's experimental system of government by law and the delicate balance of power between chieftains gradually came apart as they vied increasingly violently for influence and power during what was subsequently termed the Sturlunga Age. Brutal feuds were fought out. Even small armies were mustered and a single sea battle was fought as part of the drive for power, all in a tiny society that simply couldn't continue to support the lifestyles of its more prominent citizens. Eventually the kings of Norway stepped in and in 1262 nominally took power, later passing it to the Danish crown, and Iceland remained a colonial backwater of Denmark's little empire into the twentieth century.

There's still an undertow of rancour towards Denmark that has faded through the years. Danish was the official language and is still taught in schools, although there are few Icelanders past school age these days who could count beyond twenty in Danish, while English has become the language of business and has been adopted by Icelanders with their characteristic enthusiasm. Incidentally, Danish took a big hit when the Donald Duck comics that every child used to read before the days of cable TV were finally translated into Icelandic. Kids no longer had to read Danish to find out what Donald, Daisy and Uncle Scrooge were up to.

Iceland stayed in the dark ages far longer than the rest of Europe, smitten by natural disasters such as the Lákagígar eruption in 1783–84, which is thought to have killed six million people worldwide as the vented poisonous gases circled the globe and caused droughts and famines. In Iceland the eruption is reckoned to have killed off half the livestock and a quarter of the population. The Eyjafjallajökull eruption that grounded aircraft across the northern hemisphere in 2010 was a cough and a sneeze by comparison. As a Danish colony, Iceland was largely held back until the beginning of the twentieth century, when business became less restricted and townships began to swell to an appreciable size. But it was when the Second World War broke out and Iceland was occupied, first by British troops and later by American ones, that things began to change as the foreign money began to flow. Iceland became a state in its own right as independence from then-Nazi-occupied Denmark was achieved, and after the war Marshall Aid brought tractors and trucks, and roads began to be built. The last villages and hamlets that were only reachable by boat or on horseback were hauled into the twentieth century.

In a remarkably few years Iceland became a thoroughly prosperous country. There was work for those who wanted it, mainly in the fishing business, which was always in need of a little extra manpower to fillet and freeze or salt the fish. The trade in fish ensured that Iceland remained largely immune to the swings in economies elsewhere in Europe, and the last time that Icelanders saw hard times was in the late 1960s, when the Atlanto-Scandian herring abruptly disappeared, the victim partly of heavy fishing but also of natural fluctuations in fish stocks and climatic changes. But the hard times didn't last long. Fishing switched to groundfish, notably cod, and the fishing fleet grew as a couple of Cod Wars were fought to kick out the mainly British and German trawlers. To skip over the convoluted details of fish politics, the Cod Wars were more than likely won behind the scenes as NATO could hardly have two of its members squabbling over fish when the US air base at Keflavík, crucial to the Cold War effort, could have been at stake. As the British and German trawlers retreated, Icelandic owners ramped up their own fishing efforts and were soon landing as much as the foreigners had been doing before. The next step ushered in an age of quotas and restrictions that endures to this day, still providing one of the main undercurrents of division within Icelandic society.

It didn't take long for Iceland to be transformed from a society based on farming and fishing to a consumer society, complete with all the right toys. The distance from Europe and America, the proximity to nature, the toughness of their forebears, and the elemental nature of a society centred on producing rather than trade has given Icelanders a frontier mentality. Pleasures are taken while they're there, while new crazes are eagerly leapt upon and gobbled up wholeheartedly. Icelanders have a mind-set all of their own, although it could also be argued that Iceland has become almost two nations, the Reykjavík region and the rest of the country, which have very different and distinctive attitudes towards pretty much everything.

The 1990s saw Iceland go wild. The economy boomed. Shopping malls were built that were big enough for every inhabitant of Iceland, Greenland and the Faroe Islands to all go shopping at once. Regulation of business was severely out of fashion as the right-leaning government slackened off the leash.

At the same time the government pushed through fundamental changes to the fishing quota legislation that had been enacted almost a decade earlier, effectively making fishing rights as close as they could be to being private property. Opposed at the time by both politicians and organisations, the move made fish quotas sellable, leasable and, crucially, mortgageable via roundabout routes. This change has been seen almost as a forerunner to the decision to privatise the three partially state-owned banks around 2000, ushering in an intense spell of financial lunacy that saw the crash finally take place in 2008.

It was only a few years before those privatised banks collapsed during those strange weeks in October 2008. In fact, 2008 was the year everything went wrong for Iceland. I lived there for many years, have roots that run deep into the rocks and visit frequently, so it hasn't been a painless experience watching things coming tumbling down so dramatically. With hindsight, it should all have been so obvious. There were a few people who predicted doom and were laughed down. Others asked where all that money came from and where it was going and found themselves vilified from the highest level. Some of us had our doubts, saw the number of high-rises going up and the private jets taking off, suspecting it must have been all done with smoke and mirrors, but kept quiet.

I was in Iceland for a few days at the beginning of 2008 to do some research for a book and to look up old friends. It was cold, there was snow on the ground, and Reykjavík wasn't all that inviting, but it was business as usual. Iceland was its usual ebullient, hyperactive, overenthusiastic self. A few months later and into spring, there was a subtle change in the air. The currency had tumbled and it was an open secret that the banks weren't lending anymore. The construction business had already ground to a halt, and much else was quietly winding down. Another month down the line and the word was that the banks weren't lending because there was nothing in their coffers to lend.

Emerging from the Crash

What was spooky about it was that everything was whispered. The media and government blustered and told the world and each other that everything was fine, as if nothing could possibly be wrong. It's still unclear exactly how much the government really knew about what was happening under its nose, or if those running the country knew there was nothing they could do and just decided to brazen it out after having left things too late for a change of course.

While nothing was said out loud, every factory foreman, truck driver, hairdresser and plumber knew that something wasn't right. The flow of money and business had slowed right down. Things weren't getting done. Companies weren't able to walk into banks that had been overflowing with cash and borrow to support their normal work schedules. Work was drying up. Suddenly, keeping to a budget was critical. But still nobody said anything too loudly, waiting for something to happen without knowing quite what, or when, or how much of a blow it was going to be. The key indicator was that a good half of the Poles upped sticks and left. Iceland had seen a massive influx of foreign labour, particularly Eastern Europeans working in construction and manufacturing, but as the Icelandic currency lost value, many of them immediately left for the Eurozone countries, where a better living could be had.

In October 2008 I arrived in Iceland on an autumn evening, this time for a work trip that meant spending a few days at a trade fair. On the following morning the news was announced that Glitnir, one of Iceland's three overheated banks, had not been able to meet its commitments.

"Congratulate me on my bank," an old friend said when we met that afternoon.

"Your bank?"

"Glitnir's been bailed out by the government. So that makes it a state bank. I pay my taxes, so that means I own it now."

"Part of it, surely?"

"Well, yeah. But you know what I mean."

It was a very uncomfortable week. The trade fair was awkward, buzzing with rumours and uncertainty. The other two banks were on the brink of collapse, and then they weren't. Then Kaupthing was going to weather the storm, but Landsbanki was going to crash, or the other way around. There were stands at the fair that were empty as companies were immediately in turmoil. Everyone was wondering if they would still have a job next week. The three banks, all big lenders to industry, had significant presences, big stands manned at the last minute by skeleton crews of junior staff who presumably couldn't answer any questions because none of them knew anything anyway.

Iceland was stunned. Looking back now, it seems that nobody knew quite what was happening. When anti-terrorist legislation was used by the UK authorities as part of its actions towards Landsbanki, there was universal disbelief, followed by outrage. This was the stuff that made Icelanders stick together. The overseas banking schemes run by Landsbanki and Kaupthing in Holland and the UK became the focal point of the issue, with the British and Dutch governments cast as the demons, rather than the banks that had engineered the too-good-to-be-true high-interest schemes to start with.

The authorities seemed bewildered, first by what was happening and then by what wasn't. Iceland found to its surprise that its friends were actually few and far between. There had been a fond belief that there was a special relationship with the US, not least when the Icelandic government decided to support the Iraq War without a debate in Parliament on the subject. That confidence had already been partially shattered when the US closed its airbase at Keflavík, no longer needed once the Cold War had long since thawed out. Most likely it hurt when it wasn't George Bush himself who let the Prime Minister know but instead someone considerably junior who called to say thanks and goodbye at short notice. Talk of a super-loan from Russia turned out to be hot air. Ideas of adopting either the Norwegian krone or the Canadian dollar as a replacement for Iceland's beleaguered currency likewise came to nothing. Only neighbours in the tiny Faroe Islands, who had gone through the national trauma of their own financial meltdown in the 1990s, came unconditionally to Iceland's aid.

A new government was swept to power in the spring following the crash—that week in October having now become a pivotal point in Iceland's modern history—following the first outpourings of popular anger seen for fifty or more years as fires were lit outside Parliament, eggs were thrown at the windows, and upturned oil drums were hammered through winter nights. This was the first centre-left government the country had seen for decades, elected with a relatively slim majority as an uneasy coalition, and it was immediately handed a whole load of poisoned chalices. Under Jóhanna Sigurðardóttir, a well-respected Social Democrat and Iceland's first female and openly gay premier, the post-crash government was in many ways doomed to fail, opposed at every single turn by right-wing parties that had found themselves in opposition for practically the first time in living memory, and beset by problems that stubbornly remained beyond its ability to handle. It didn't help that the two government parties had wildly different agendas on Europe, with the Social Democrats determined to drag Iceland into the European Union while their Left-Green bedfellows were firmly against it but allowed themselves to be horse-traded into it.

The right wing had taken its election defeat hard and concentrated on gaining every advantage going towards winning the next election, sniping from the sidelines at every opportunity and fighting a desperate rear-guard action during its final days in office. During twenty-odd years in power, and in spite of pressure from within its own ranks, it had never found the right moment to license whaling. Yet with a few hours to go before handing over the keys, one outgoing minister signed the forms and licensed a fin whale hunt, presumably knowing that there would be an international outcry that his successor would have to deal with.

Of the books written about Iceland in the last century or so, one of the most interesting is *Letters from Iceland*, a travelogue written by poets Louis MacNeice and W.H. Auden when they travelled around parts of the country just before the Second World War, back when Iceland was still a Danish backwater reached by steamship. Auden wrote at one point, "I understand local politics are very corrupt." Not much has changed on that score in the intervening seventy-five years. Politics, business, the media, and the judiciary are all uncomfortably bound together by discreet allegiances, unspoken sympathies, political ties and family bonds in a country so small that conflicts of interest can hardly be avoided and are frequently either shrugged off or accepted as a fact of life.

It has been a long haul for Icelanders since those mad months at the end of 2008. There is a huge amount of wounded pride and frustration over the failure both to deal with the consequences of the crash and to delve into the causes of it, although the latter process has made uncomfortable progress through the efforts of the Special Prosecutor's office and the deeply incongruous spectacle of former Prime Minister Geir Haarde's impeachment. That resulted in his being convicted on one count but with no penalty imposed on him. The odd thing about this was the series of members of former and present governments who all claimed to have known nothing—though in any case, they insisted, there was nothing they could have done—made even more strange by the fact that Geir Haarde was on his own in the dock as other senior ministers in his administration were not indicted. Maybe the performance was expected to have had some cathartic effect on Iceland's riven society. If that was the case, it certainly didn't succeed, but it made for some riveting news.

Then there's the fish issue, which still hasn't gone away and isn't likely to. The post-crash centre-left government came to power on the strength of their not being the conservative wide boys who had created the environment for the banking sector to mushroom to a dozen times the country's GDP, as well as with a clear mandate to reform fisheries management, a prospect so divisive that in previous elections there had supposedly been gentlemen's agreements not to raise the quota issue. But after almost twenty years of not being addressed, fisheries are at the core of the divisions in Icelandic society. The big hitters of the established interests rolled out their heaviest artillery in what has become a propaganda war that is set to run between the quota holders on one side and a large swath of the general public on the other. It's an ill-defined, skewed debate that pits the deeply conservative "countryside"—the term used to refer to the entire country outside the Reykjavík area—against the city dwellers (not that this is exclusively the case).

Much of the rancour between "the South," as the Reykjavík region is known colloquially, and the "countryside" stems from the population drift towards the city and the overwhelming need to seek goods and services there as everything is increasingly concentrated around Reykjavík. Need new glasses or new teeth? You'll probably have to go down south for that.

The quota furore has been at the centre of the population drift that has left many smaller settlements denuded of employment as tradable fishing quotas went to the highest bidders. Quotas change hands in a process that accumulates fishing rights in increasingly fewer hands, and much the same trends have been seen in many other countries, including Chile, New Zealand, Namibia and some EU nations, all of which followed the basic model that Iceland pioneered all those years ago.

One result is a streamlined, efficient fishing business, but a side effect is that places that were once thriving communities went from being bustling coastal villages to being virtually abandoned. Ships stayed at the quayside, factories closed, and people drifted away to where work could still be found, sometimes leaving behind a suddenly worthless property that half a lifetime of work had gone into.

But the fisheries issue is only half of the story. Iceland's rural and coastal areas have seen a migration "south" for the best part of a century that accelerated as the opportunities became fewer elsewhere. Reykjavík is quite simply more exciting. It's a small city with bars and nightclubs, more variety of work and plenty of shopping opportunities instead of the single Co-op or equivalent that many smaller places have. Educational institutions in Iceland are located largely in Reykjavík, and the universal phenomenon of graduates going away to study and never returning has taken much of the younger generation south and increasingly abroad. Many of the children of the generation that found outlying towns and villages too small for them thirty years ago have since found Reykjavík too parochial and have chosen to take themselves to London or Copenhagen—not least in the wake of the crash.

So is Iceland recovering, as has been reported so widely overseas, particularly in the light of the Greek and Irish financial crises? It's very hard to tell. Business may be slowly gaining ground. Reykjavík's shopping malls seem busy enough, and the smarter boutiques and restaurants haven't disappeared. The wealthy are still wealthy. A good few of the Porsche-owning, football club-buying financial whiz-kids who may or may not have been instrumental in causing the crash are able to live in Reykjavík, bizarrely without being assaulted, although the worst excesses of the boom years have been severely toned down. It's no longer the done thing to be wildly ostentatious. "That's just so 2007" is the derisive expression used to describe anything flashily over the top. But personal debt is still vast, and unemployment remains uncomfortably high by Icelandic standards, though the level would not be close to high on a Spanish or Greek scale.

Much of the "countryside" is still living in the recession and has been in gradual decline for the best part of the last twenty years, so there are no big changes there. It's Reykjavík that has borne the brunt of the crash. Maybe contrary to popular belief, there is poverty in Iceland. It's something that had hardly existed a few years before, and today those people are certainly no better off than they were. Those who seem to be hit hardest appear to be middle Iceland: the hard-working, loan-taking, hard-spending types who keep business and the economy afloat—and these are the people who are also forming the largest emigration of Icelanders since the disappearance of the herring forty years before.

An Icelandic diaspora has begun to take shape, although most have gone to Scandinavia, primarily to Norway, with a great many skilled, highly educated professionals leaving for greener pastures as Iceland's public services, from health care to education to garbage collection, have all been slashed to the bone and beyond.

During the height of the spending spree, a massive new project was begun: the construction of a world-class concert and conference centre on the shoreside in Reykjavík. For a country where fishing is so important, it seemed somehow wrong to see Reykjavík's modern fish auction torn down and relocated to a fifty-year-old building on the unfashionable side of the harbour. The construction was backed by one of the business moguls and largely funded by his bank, and when the banks ground to a standstill, so did the opera house project, leaving a half-completed shell in its incongruous setting.

There was a long debate about what to do with the place, and eventually it was finished, with the city and the state jumping in to foot the bill. It's in a bizarre setting, right next to the busiest street in the country, over the road from the Central Bank that had failed dismally to keep tabs on the bankers to start with.

There aren't any quick fixes or silver bullets for Iceland, although that's undoubtedly what Icelanders would like to see. It has taken the country a couple of generations since independence to become a buzzing, vibrant society with all the luxuries and trappings of consumerism on display. But without the necessary brakes put on its madcap financial sector, and with the corruption that Auden mentioned in passing before the war, it could easily take another generation for Iceland to emerge from its new Sturlunga Age of intrigue and power struggles and get back on its feet again.

But the glittering glass frontage of the opera house, now named Harpa, is there on the edge of the city overlooking the sea and the mountains beyond, a permanent reminder of just how badly things can go wrong—as well as an indicator of what can be achieved when they go right.

Quentin Bates

Quentin Bates escaped English suburbia as a teenager, after which his gap year in Iceland gradually became a gap decade, acquiring a family, a new language and sea legs as a trawlerman. These days he lives in England and writes, but Iceland still calls and is never far away.

Shaking the Hand That Shook the Hand: A Footnote to Orwell

George Fetherling

My mentor's mentor was George Orwell. His name was George Woodcock, and he was an author widely known in Canada, where he was born and spent the larger portion of his life. Before that, in his late twenties and early thirties—the years during and either side of the Second World War—he had been a rising literary figure in Britain. Specifically, he was a member of what at least in retrospect seems an important if loosely organised group of left-wing writers and critics of whom Orwell was another. By the time of his death, in Vancouver in 1995, aged eighty-two, Woodcock had published nearly 150 works of history, poetry, narrative travel, biography, memoir, and social and cultural criticism. Several of these books resonate clearly in the Canadian consciousness. An example is *Gabriel Dumont: The Métis Chief and His Lost World* (1975), a biography of the military leader of the North-West Rebellion, an 1885 uprising against the Dominion government. Woodcock's two most widely read works, however, are of an international character. The first, *Anarchism: A History of Libertarian Ideas and*

Movements, did much to educate the New Left of the 1960s and is still in print fifty years later. The other is *The Crystal Spirit: A Study of George Orwell*. It appeared in 1966.

Woodcock was nine years younger than Orwell: a difference almost but not quite large enough to keep them from being contemporaries as well as mere coevals. The greater disparity was in their social class and related world view. Orwell of course was an old Etonian who, as we all know, later entered the colonial service in Burma. He never quite lost the expensively acquired posh accent, but he soon discarded imperial doctrine and any conservative viewpoint he might have had. Woodcock attended only a minor school, and then on merit, not money, and never studied at a university. He was reared mostly in the Thames Valley. From many years until 1940, he commuted to London to work as a minor railway clerk in the offices above Paddington Station. As some of his very earliest writings show, he was a radical from the beginning, steeped in the history of the left.

Not surprisingly, the Second World War had some profound effects on literary London. For one thing, the war effort put many writers into uniform. For another, it imposed paper rationing. Paradoxically, the latter fact, though it led to a decrease in new books being published, seemed to help spur greater demand for reading material of all kinds. For example, newsagents, and also the railway bookstalls so important to British book culture, began stocking small literary magazines. One of these was *NOW*, which Woodcock had begun editing in 1940 as a vehicle for political dissenters of all stripes: anarchists, socialists, pacifists and, on the anti-authoritarian right, libertarians (a different use of the word from that found in the subtitle to Woodcock's *Anarchism*). Contributors included Herbert (later Sir Herbert) Read, the art critic and anarchist, the poet Roy Campbell, and the anarchist and gerontologist Alex Comfort (famous to a later generation for writing *The Joy of Sex*). There were also a few American writers such as Henry Miller and Kenneth Rexroth, for another result of the odd wartime atmosphere was that literary Britain and literary America grew less incomprehensible to each other and, indeed, more hospitable.

So it was that Orwell began to contribute a "London Letter" for the most important of US intellectual journals, the *Partisan Review*. In one of these letters he excoriated Woodcock for his pacifism (he became a conscientious objector but later deserted the CO system and went underground) and for opening *NOW* to anti-authoritarian rightists. Woodcock, who by coincidence was in the process of writing an essay on Orwell's work, reacted with the usual criticism of Orwell's elitist education and history of colonial service. Orwell responded by inviting him to come to Broadcasting House, where he was producing radio programmes for the audience in India. There is a frequently reproduced photograph of Orwell, Woodcock, Read, the poet-critics William Empson and Edmund Blunden, and the Indian novelist Mulk Raj Anand in the studio, gathered round a BBC microphone.

Woodcock's father had gone out to Canada in 1907 to make a success of himself, eventually sending for his family. Hence George's birth in Winnipeg. Ultimately, they all returned to Britain in failure, and the father, Arthur Woodcock, died young. During the wartime period, Woodcock once told me, he "was constantly searching" for a father, perhaps a "shaman-father." In 1942, he met two of them: Read and Orwell. They "became jointly the wise father as far as I was concerned, and I loved both of them, though with British reticence I never said anything about it." When he said this I realised that my friendship with him was essentially like that of his to Orwell. I found comfort in that situation, which neither of us spoke of openly to each other.

In such situations as that of Woodcock and Orwell, personality plays an even bigger role than politics. Looked at in one way, the fellow member of the ring with whom Woodcock would appear on the surface to have the most in common was Kenneth Rexroth, the San Francisco poet, polymath—and anarchist. They reached their literary adulthood in the 1930s. The betrayals of the Spanish Civil War affected them deeply. Both were not only conscientious objectors during the Second World War but also victims of McCarthyism afterwards. Rexroth, however, was a toxic personality, infamously so. As for Orwell, although he was never an anarchist, he shared with Woodcock a rich fund of political ideas. Once he had resettled back in Canada, Woodcock turned away from most anarchist activity to concentrate on literary work (including a number of works on anarchist history). By changing this way, he found himself in a political position even closer to Orwell's. As life in Canada rolled on, Orwell became, much more so than Read, the wise father—significantly, the wise dead father, who could be idealised without fear of contradiction. On arriving in Vancouver in 1950 Woodcock found that the great love of his life, his anarchist colleague Marie Louise Berneri, had died. Shortly afterwards came news of Orwell's death. For the rest of his life, Woodcock referred to Orwell's works and ideas more than those of any other writer, including even Prince Kropotkin (1842-1921), the person who made anarchism into an *ism*—a philosophy rather than a hodgepodge of theories, ideas and notions.

Orwell set the standard of intellectual honesty against which Woodcock would measure his own performance for the rest of his life. Talking with me once about the Spanish Civil War, he said: "The writers I was associated with in the 1940s kept the faith in their individual ways, but *all* were disillusioned with the Communist role there. We salvaged the Spanish communes for history, and I wrote about them, but as events in the past. Books like *Homage to Catalonia* were really denunciations and threnodies combined. No one in my circle 'kept faith with the left' if by that you mean the CPGB [Communist Party of Great Britain] which bemused so many writers of the 1930s."

The Crystal Spirit is a book that required considerable diplomacy. Woodcock had been writing prolifically about Orwell for audiences on both sides of the Atlantic—writing about his politics, his ideas and his art—when in 1955 he approached the notoriously difficult widow, Sonia Bronwell Orwell, about the possibility of writing a biography. She refused, as she had been appointing various prominent authors to undertake the task—phantom biographers, at least six of them in sequence, whose projects would be announced to keep the vultures away but would never actually get written. After tortuous negotiations through third parties, Woodcock got her permission to write a book about her husband and to quote from his writings, if it were mainly a work of literary criticism. Accordingly, this, the first of so many books about George Orwell, was one part memoir to three parts criticism—but with the ingredients mixed so skillfully as to disguise the recipe. It remains, in my view, an artful and fascinating piece of work, one of those books that the person who wrote it simply had to undertake, as though under some sub-divine obligation.

Reading it leaves one with the impression that Orwell may have been the first important postwar British civilian writer on whom all the civilian scars of the war showed plainly. Like most skilled journalists (this is one of their chief faults) he was stuck in the present, preferring it to either of the alternatives. Woodcock's personal reminiscences of Orwell paint him as a person for whom the bad times had the virtue of being real times. The times in question tended to make a mockery of the old imperialist ideas of which he disapproved. They tended to show the stupidity of class disparity, which he disliked because it was so destructive—and also because he too was, in his way, its victim.

After leaving the BBC, Orwell went to work as the book review editor of *Tribune*, the left-wing weekly, then located in unprepossessing offices in the Strand. Woodcock would visit him there, and later could remember the sound of V2 rockets whining over the city as they talked. Food was being rationed. Instead of complaining about what was available to eat, Orwell tried to convince himself and others that the hardship was actually a delight. Woodcock recalled one lunch at which his friend tucked into boiled cod and turnip tops— the only dishes available that day—with enthusiasm, as though he were contemplating writing an essay entitled How the Poor Eat. He poured tea into his saucer and blew on it before drinking. But the pose didn't fool anyone. Orwell made one of his few public speeches at an event to raise funds for Marie Louise Berneri and other anarchists to be tried at the Old Bailey on a charge of spreading "disaffection" among the troops. Such an act was testament to Orwell's belief in free speech, because the throat wound he received in Spain had left his voice much less well-modulated than before. But he still had the posh accent and, in Woodcock's phrase, "always looked the tired English sahib in his shabby old sportscoat." Also apparent was the tuberculosis that would kill him. When the Woodcocks (George had married Ingeborg Roskelly, a fierce eccentric who ran every aspect of his existence for the next forty-five years) were living in Highgate West Hill, N6, in 1943, Orwell would pay visits, wheezing up three flights of stairs.

When the first money arrived from *Animal Farm* (he didn't live to see a farthing from *Nineteen Eight-Four*), he took Woodcock to an expensive restaurant to celebrate. Mimicking the habits of working-class people for whom his admiration was unrequited, Orwell slipped off his jacket and hung it over the back of the chair, encouraging Woodcock to do the same. After dinner they stopped at a pub. But in that environment no one felt required to ignore Orwell's new working-class mannerisms. "The publican called us a couple of toffs," Woodcock told me, laughing, "and that was the end of that."

Orwell was stuck between social classes, as one might become trapped between floors in a lift.

George Fetherling

George Fetherling is a Canadian novelist, poet and cultural commentator. He has also written a biography, *The Gentle Anarchist: A Life of George Woodcock* (Subway Books). He lives in Vancouver and Toronto.